Orchid:
A Belle

Ace reporter Matthew Bates's
investigative instincts
were always right on target,
until he set his sights on
Laurel Armand. She was the
loveliest belle in Louisiana—
and she was in danger of losing
her life....

KU-626-132

NORA ROBERTS
LANGUAGE OF LOVE

Love has a language all its own, and for
centuries, flowers have symbolized
love's finest expression.
Discover the language of flowers
—and love—
in this romantic collection of 48 favorite
books by bestselling author Nora Roberts.

NORA ROBERTS

LANGUAGE OF LOVE

PARTNERS

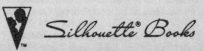

Silhouette® Books

Published by Silhouette Books New York

America's Publisher of Contemporary Romance

If you purchased this book without a cover you should be aware
that this book is stolen property. It was reported as "unsold and
destroyed" to the publisher, and neither the author nor the
publisher has received any payment for this "stripped book."

For Bruce, who changed my plans.

SILHOUETTE BOOKS
300 East 42nd St., New York, N.Y. 10017

PARTNERS © 1985 by Nora Roberts.
First published as a Silhouette Intimate Moments.

Language of Love edition published December 1992

ISBN: 0-373-51021-7

All rights reserved. Except for use in any review,
the reproduction or utilization of this work in
whole or in part in any form by any electronic,
mechanical or other means, now known or
hereafter invented, including xerography,
photocopying and recording, or in any information
storage or retrieval system, is forbidden without
the permission of the publisher, Silhouette Books,
300 E. 42nd Street, New York, N.Y. 10017

All the characters in this book have no existence
outside the imagination of the author and have
no relation whatsoever to anyone bearing the same
name or names. They are not even distantly
inspired by any individual known or unknown
to the author, and all incidents are pure invention.

® are Trademarks registered in the United States Patent
and Trademark Office, the Canada Trade Mark Office
and in other countries.

Printed in U.S.A.

Chapter One

Bedlam. Phones rang continuously. People shouted, muttered or swore, sitting or on the run. Typewriter keys clattered at varying paces from every direction. There was the scent of old coffee, fresh bread, tobacco smoke and human sweat. An insane asylum? Several of the inmates would have agreed with that description of the city room of the *New Orleans Herald,* especially at deadline.

For most of the staff the chaos went unnoticed, as the inhaling and exhaling of air went unnoticed. There were times when each one of them was too involved with their own daily crises or triumphs to be aware of the dozens of others springing up around them. Not that teamwork was ignored. All were bound, by love for, or obsession with, their jobs, in the exclusive community of journalists. Still each would concentrate on, and greedily guard, his or her own story, own sources and own style. A successful print reporter thrives on pressure and confusion and a hot lead.

Matthew Bates had cut his teeth on newsprint. He'd worked it from every angle from newsboy on the Lower East Side of Manhattan to feature reporter. He'd carried coffee, run copy, written obituaries and covered flower shows.

The ability to scent out a story and draw the meat from it wasn't something he'd learned in his journalism courses; he'd been born with it. His years of structured classes, study and practice had honed the style and technique of a talent that was as inherent as the color of his eyes.

At the age of thirty, Matt was casually cynical but not without humor for life's twists and turns. He liked people without having illusions about them. He understood and accepted that humans were basically ridiculous. How else could he work in a room full of crazy people in a profession that constantly exposed and exploited the human race?

Finishing a story, he called out for a copy boy, then leaned back to let his mind rest for the first time in three hours. A year ago, he'd left New York to accept the position on the *Herald,* wanting, perhaps needing, a change. Restless, he thought now. He'd been restless for... something. And New Orleans was as hard and demanding a town as New York, with more elegant edges.

He worked the police beat and liked it. It was a tough world, and murder and desperation were parts of it that couldn't be ignored. The homicide he'd just covered had been senseless and cruel. It had been life; it had been news. Now, he wiped the death of the eighteen-year-old girl out of his mind. Objectivity came first, unless he wanted to try a new profession. Yet it took a concentrated effort to erase her image and her ending from his mind.

He hadn't the looks of a seasoned, hard-boiled reporter, and he knew it. It had exasperated him in his twenties that he looked more like a carefree surfer than a newsman. Now, it amused him.

He had a lean, subtly muscled body that was more at home in jeans than a three-piece suit, with a height that only added a feeling of ranginess. His dark blond hair curled as it chose, over his ears, down to the collar of his shirt. It merely added to the image of a laid-back, easygoing male who'd rather be sitting on the beach than pounding the pavement. More than one source had talked freely to the façade without fully comprehending the man beneath the image. When and if they did, Matt already had the story.

When he chose, he could be charming, even elegant. But the good-humored blue eyes could turn to fire or, more dangerous, ice. Beneath the easy exterior was a cold, hard determination and a smoldering temper. Matt accepted this with a shrug. He was human, and entitled to be ridiculous.

With a half smile lingering around his mouth, he turned to the woman seated across from him. Laurel Armand— with a face as romantic as her name. She had an aura of delicacy that came from fine bones and an ivory skin that made a man want to touch, and touch gently. Her hair fell in clouds of misty black, swept back from her face, spilling onto her shoulders. Hair made for a man to dive his fingers into, bury his face in. Her eyes were the color of emeralds, dark and rich.

It was the face of a nineteenth-century belle whose life revolved around gracious indolence and quiet gentility. And her voice was just as feminine, Matt mused. It turned vowels into liquid and smoothed consonants. It never flattened, never twanged, but flowed like a leisurely stream.

The voice, he reflected as his smile widened, was just as deceptive as the face. The lady was a sharp ambitious reporter with a stubborn streak and a flaring temper. One of his favorite pastimes was setting a match to it.

Her brows were drawn together as she finished the last line of her copy. Satisfied, Laurel whipped the sheet from her typewriter, called for a copy boy, then focused on the man across from her. Automatically, her spine straightened. She already knew he was going to bait her, and that—damn it—she would bite.

"Do you have a problem, Matthew?" Her tone was soft and faintly bored.

"No problem, Laurellie." He watched the annoyance flare into her eyes at his use of her full name.

"Don't you have a murder or armed robbery to go play with?"

His mouth curved, charmingly, deepening the creases in his face. "Not at the moment. Off your soapbox for the day?"

She gritted her teeth on a spate of furious words. He never failed to dig for the emotion that seeped into her work, and she never failed to defend it. Not this time, Laurel told herself as she balled her hands into fists under her desk. "I leave the cynicism to you, Matthew," she returned with a sweetness belied by the daggers in her eyes. "You're so good at it."

"Yeah. How about a bet on whose story makes page one?"

She lifted one fragile, arched brow—a gesture he particularly admired. "I wouldn't want to take your money, Matthew."

"I don't mind taking yours." Grinning, he rose to walk around their desk and bend down to her ear. "Five bucks, magnolia blossom. Even though your papa owns the paper, our editors know the difference between reporting and crusading."

He felt the heat rise, heard the soft hiss of breath. It was tempting, very tempting, to crush his mouth onto those soft, pouting lips and taste the fury. Even as the need worked into him, Matt reminded himself that wasn't the way to outwit her.

"You're on, Bates, but make it ten." Laurel stood. It infuriated her that she had to tilt her head back to meet his eyes. It infuriated her more that the eyes were confident, amused and beautiful. Laurel fell back on the habit of imagining him short, rotund and balding. "Unless that's too rich for your blood," she added.

"Anything to oblige, love." He curled the tips of her hair around his finger. "And to prove even Yankees have chivalry, I'll buy you lunch with my winnings."

She smiled at him, leaning a bit closer so that their bodies just brushed. Matt felt the surprising jolt of heat shoot straight through his system. "When hell freezes over," Laurel told him, then shoved him aside.

Matt watched her storm away; then, dipping his hands into his pockets, he laughed. In the confusion of the city room, no one noticed.

"Damn!" Laurel swore as she maneuvered her car through the choking downtown traffic. Matthew Bates was the most irritating man she'd ever known. Squeezing through on an amber light, she cursed fate. If her brother Curt hadn't met him in college, Matthew would never have accepted the position on the *Herald.* Then he'd be insufferable in New York instead of being insufferable two feet away from her day after day.

Honesty forced her to admit, even when it hurt, that he was the best reporter on the staff. He was thorough, insightful and had the instincts of a bloodhound. But that didn't make him any easier to swallow. Laurel hit the brakes and swerved as a Buick cut her off. She was too annoyed with Matt to be bothered by traffic warfare.

His piece on the homicide had been clean, concise and excellent. She wished she'd stuffed the ten dollars down his throat. That would've made it difficult for him to gloat over it.

In the twelve months she'd known and worked with him, he'd never reacted toward her as other men did. There was no deference in him, no admiration in his eyes. The fact that she despised being deferred to didn't make her resent him any less.

He'd never asked her out—not that she wanted him to, Laurel reminded herself firmly. Except for missing the pure pleasure of turning him down. Even though he'd moved into her apartment building, virtually next door to her, he'd never come knocking at her door on the smallest of pretenses. For a year she'd been hoping he would—so she could slam the door in his face.

What he did, she thought as she gritted her teeth, was make a nuisance of himself in a dozen other ways. He made cute little observations on her dates—all the more irritating because they were invariably true. These days his favorite target was Jerry Cartier, an ultraconservative, somewhat dense city councilman. Laurel saw him because she was too kindhearted not to, and he occasionally gave her a lead. But Matt put her in the intolerable position of having to defend Jerry against her own opinion.

Life would be simpler, she thought, if Matthew Bates were still hustling newsprint in Manhattan. And if he weren't so impossibly attractive. Laurel blocked Matt, and her ten dollars, out of her mind as she left the traffic behind.

Though the sun was hanging low, the sky was still brilliant. Warmth and light filtered through the cypresses and streamed onto the road. Deep in the trees were shadows and the musical sound of insects and birds, creatures of the marsh. She'd always known there were secrets in the marshes. Secrets, shadows, dangers. They only added to the beauty. There was something exciting in knowing another way of life thrived—primitive, predatory—so near civilization.

As she turned into the lane that led to her ancestral home, Laurel felt the familiar mix of pride and tranquility. Cedars guarded each side of the drive, arching overhead to transform the lane into a cool, dim tunnel. The sun filtered through sporadically, throwing patches of light on the ground. Spanish moss dripped from the branches to add that timeless grace so peculiar to the South. As she traveled down the drive of Promesse d'Amour, the clock turned back. Life was easy.

At the end of the drive, Laurel stopped to look at the house. There were two rambling stories of white-washed brick surrounded by a profusion of azaleas, camellias and magnolias. The colors, vivid and delicate, the scents, exotic and gentle, added to the sense of antebellum style and indolence. With the window down, she could smell the mix of heat and fragrance.

There were twenty-eight Doric columns that added dignity rather than ostentation. Ivy clung to each corner post. The grillwork on the encircling balcony was as delicate as black lace and French doors led to it from every room. The effect of the house was one of durability, security and grace. Laurel saw it as a woman who had coped with the years and emerged with character and gentility. If the house had been flesh and blood, she couldn't have loved it more.

She took the side steps to the porch and entered without knocking. Her childhood had been spent there, her girlhood, her adolescence. A wide hallway split the building in two, running from front door to back. Lingering in the air was the scent of bee's wax and lemon, to mix with the fragrance from a bowl of camellia blossoms. The hall would have held the same scent a century before. Laurel paused only briefly in front of a cheval glass to brush the hair away from her face before she walked into the front parlor.

"Hello, papa." She went to him, rising on her toes to kiss a cheek rough from a day's growth of beard. William Armand was lanky and handsome with dark hair just hinting at gray. While he ran his daily paper with verve, temper and tenacity, he chose an easier pace for his personal life. He smelled of good whiskey and tobacco. In an old habit, he mussed the hair Laurel had just straightened.

"Hello, princess. Good story on the mayor." He lifted a brow in puzzlement as he saw the quick flash of irritation in her eyes.

"Thanks." She smiled so quickly, her father thought he'd imagined that dangerous light. Turning, she studied the woman who sat in a royal blue tufted chair.

The hair was pure white, but as full and thick as Laurel's. It surrounded a face layered and lined with wrinkles and unashamedly rouged. Olivia Armand wasn't ashamed of anything. Eyes as sharp and green as the emeralds in her ears studied Laurel in turn.

"Grandma." With a sigh, Laurel bent to kiss her. "Will you never grow old?"

"Not if I have anything to say about it." Her voice was raspy with age and stunningly sensual. "You're the same," she continued, taking Laurel's hand in her strong, dry one. "It's good Creole blood." After giving Laurel's hand a quick squeeze, she sat back in her chair. "William, fix the child a drink and top mine off while you're at it. How's your love life these days, Laurellie?"

Grinning, Laurel dropped down on the hassock at her grandmother's feet. "Not as varied as yours." She caught her father's wink as he handed her a glass.

"Hogwash!" Olivia tossed back her bourbon. "I'll tell you what's wrong with the world today, too much business and not enough romance. Your problem, Laurel-lie"—she paused to jab a finger at her granddaughter—"is wasting time on that spineless Cartier. Not enough blood in him to warm a woman's bed."

"Thank God," Laurel said with a grateful look at the ceiling. "That's the last place I want him."

"Time you had someone there," Olivia retorted.

Laurel lifted a brow while her father tried not to choke on his drink. "Not all of us," Laurel said smoothly, "have your, shall we say, bawdy turn of mind."

Olivia gave a hoot of laughter and smacked the arm of her chair. "Not everyone admits it, that's the difference."

Unable to resist her grandmother's outrageousness, Laurel grinned. "Curt should be here soon, shouldn't he?"

"Any minute." William eased his tall, angular frame into a chair. "He called just before you came in. He's bringing a friend with him."

"A woman, I hope," Olivia said irrepressibly before she polished off her bourbon. "Boy's got his nose stuck in too many law books. Between the two of you," she added, rounding on Laurel again, "I'll never be a great-grandmother. The pair of you're too wrapped up in law and newspapers to find a lover."

"I'm not ready to get married," Laurel said tranquilly as she held her glass up to the light.

"Who said anything about marriage?" Olivia wanted to know. Heaving a sigh, she looked at her son. "Children nowadays don't know anything."

Laurel was laughing when she heard the sound of the front door closing. "That'll be Curt. I believe I'll warn him about the frame of mind you're in."

"Damned pretty girl," Olivia muttered when Laurel strolled out.

"She's the image of you," her son commented as he lit one of his cigars.

Olivia cackled. "Damned pretty."

The moment she entered the hall, Laurel's smile faded and her jaw tensed. Her eyes flicked over her brother to the man beside him. "Oh, it's you."

Matt took her hand, raising it to his lips before Laurel could jerk it away. "Ah, southern hospitality." Good God, he thought as his gaze roamed over her, she's beautiful. All that passion, all that fire, under ivory and roses. One day, Laurellie, he promised silently, we're going to set it all loose. My way.

Ignoring the warmth that lingered on her knuckles from his lips, Laurel turned to her brother. He had the angularity and aristocratic features of their father, and the eyes of a dreamer. As Matt watched, the restrained temper on her face softened with affection.

"Hi." She put her hands on her brother's shoulders, leaving them there after she'd kissed him. "How are you?"

"Fine. Busy." He gave her an absent smile, as if he'd just remembered where he was.

"The busy might be an issue tonight," she told him with a chuckle. "Grandma's in one of her moods."

He gave her such a pained look that Laurel laughed and kissed him again. Poor Curt, she thought, so shy and sweet. Turning her head, she looked directly into Matt's eyes. He was watching her coolly, with something undefinable flickering behind the aloof expression. A tremble skidded up her spine, but she kept her eyes level. Who is he really? she wondered, not for the first time. And why, after an entire year, am I still not sure? It always puzzled her how a man with his energy, wit and cynicism should remain such good friends with her gentle, dreamy brother. It puzzled her, too, that she couldn't pin him down to a type. Perhaps that was why he invaded her thoughts so often. Involuntarily, her gaze slipped down to his mouth. It curved. Silently, she swore.

"I guess we'd better go in," Curt said, oblivious to the undercurrents around him. He smiled in a quick, boyish way that animated his soft eyes. "Having Matt along should distract her. Distracting women's one of his best talents."

Laurel gave an unladylike snort. "I'll bet."

As Curt started into the parlor, Matt took Laurel's hand and tucked it into his arm. "Another wager, Laurellie?" he murmured. "Name the stakes."

There was something insolent in the softly spoken words. She tossed her head back in an angry gesture that pleased him enormously. "If you don't let go of my hand, I'm going to—"

"Embarrass yourself," Matt finished as they crossed the threshold into the parlor.

He'd always liked the room—the faded colors and polished old wood. There were times when he was here that Matt forgot the years he'd spent in a cramped third-floor walk-up with a radiator that let off more noise than heat. That part of his life was over; he'd seen to it. Yet snatches of it crept up on him in spite of success. Shoes that were too small, a belly never quite full—an ambition that threatened to outdistance opportunity. No, he'd never take success for granted. He'd spent too many years fighting for it.

"So, you've brought the Yankee, have you?" Olivia sent Matt a sparkling look and prepared to enjoy herself.

Curt greeted his father, dutifully kissed Olivia's cheek, then busied himself mixing drinks. Grandma had that look in her eye.

"Miss Olivia." Matt took the offered hand and lifted it to his lips. "More beautiful than ever."

"Rascal," she accused, but the pleasure came through. "You haven't been to see me for a month—a dangerous amount of time at my age."

Matt kissed her hand again while his eyes laughed into hers. "I only stay away because you won't marry me."

Laurel struggled not to smile as she chose a chair across the room. Did he have to be so damned charming?

Olivia's laugh was a sound of pure, feminine appreciation. "Thirty years ago, you scoundrel, I'd have given you a chase, even if you are a Yankee."

Matt took the offered glass, and the grateful look, Curt gave him before he turned back to Olivia. "Miss Olivia, I wouldn't have run." He perched on the arm of her chair, much, Laurel thought resentfully, like a favored nephew.

"Well, the time's passed for that," she decided with a sigh before she aimed a look at Laurel. "Why haven't you taken up with this devil, Laurellie? He's a man to keep a woman's blood moving."

Color, as much from annoyance as embarrassment, rose in Laurel's cheeks as Matt sent her a wolfish grin. She sat in stony silence, cursing the fairness of her skin.

"Now that's a fine, feminine trick," her grandmother observed, tapping Matt on the thigh. "Good for the complexion, too. Why I could still call out a blush on demand after I'd had a husband and three lovers under my belt." Pleased with the deadly stare her granddaughter aimed at her, Olivia lifted her face to Matt's. "Good-looking girl, isn't she?"

"Lovely," Matt agreed, enjoying himself almost as much as Olivia was.

"Breed fine sons."

"Have another drink, mother," William suggested, observing the war signals in his daughter's eyes.

"Fine idea." She handed over her empty glass. "You haven't seen the gardens, Matthew. They're at their peak. Laurellie, take this Yankee out and show him what a proper garden looks like."

Laurel shot her grandmother an icy glare. "I'm sure Matthew—"

"Would love to," he finished for her, rising.

She switched the glare to him without any effort. "I don't—"

"Want to be rude," he supplied quietly as he helped her out of her chair.

Oh yes, she did, Laurel thought as she swung through the garden doors. She wanted very badly to be rude. But not in front of her family, and he knew it. "You really enjoy this don't you?" she hissed at him the moment the door closed behind them.

"Enjoy what?" Matt countered.

"Infuriating me."

"It's impossible not to enjoy something one's so good at."

She chuckled, then despised herself. "All right, here's the garden." She made a wide gesture. "And you don't want to see it any more than I want to show it to you."

"Wrong," Matt said simply, and took her hand again.

"Will you stop that!" Exasperated, Laurel shook her hand but failed to free it. "That's a new habit you've picked up."

"I just found out I like it." He drew her off the terrace onto one of the narrow paths that wound through the flowers. "Besides, if you don't make a good showing at this, Olivia'll just think of something else."

Too true, Laurel admitted. She'd tolerate the man beside her. After all, the sun was splashing red on the horizon and the garden smelled like paradise. It'd been too long since she'd taken the time to see it at dusk. They walked under an arched trellis with wisteria dripping like rain. The birds of the sunlight were beginning to quiet, and those of the night had yet to wake.

"I've always loved it best at this time of day," Laurel said without thinking. "You can almost see the women with their hooped skirts swishing along the edges of the paths. There'd have been musicians in the gazebo and strings of colored lanterns."

He'd known she had a streak of romance, a touch of her brother's dreaminess, but she'd been so careful not to show either to him before. Instinctively, he knew she hadn't meant to now, but the garden had weakened her. He wondered, as he trailed his thumb lightly over her knuckles, what other weaknesses she might have.

"It would've smelled the same then as it does tonight," Matt murmured, discovering just how exquisite her skin looked in the golden light of sunset. "Hot and sweet and secret."

"When I was a girl, I'd come out here sometimes at dusk and pretend I was meeting someone." The memory made her smile, a little dreamy, a little wistful. "Sometimes he'd be dark and dashing—or he'd be tall and blond, but always dangerous and unsuitable. The kind of man a young girl's papa would've whisked her away from." She laughed, letting her fingers trail over a waxy, white camellia. "Strange that I would've had those kinds of fancies when my papa knew I was much too ambitious and practical to fall for a..."

Laurel trailed off when she turned her head and found him close—so close it was his scent that aroused her senses rather than the blossom's; his breath she felt on her skin rather than the sultry evening air. The light was touched with gold, blushed with rose. Hazy, magical. In it, he looked too much like someone she might have dreamed of.

Matt let his fingers play lightly with the pulse at her wrist. It wasn't steady, but this time it wasn't anger that unsettled it. "A what?"

"A rogue," Laurel managed after a moment.

They were talking softly, as if they were telling secrets. The sun slipped lower, and the shadows lengthened.

His face was so lean, she thought suddenly. Not predatory, but the face of a man who wouldn't step aside if trouble got in his way. His eyes were guarded, but she'd noticed before how easily he concealed his thoughts. Perhaps that was why he nudged information from people without appearing to nudge at all. And his mouth—how was it she'd never realized how tempting, how sensual his mouth was? Or had she simply pretended not to? It wouldn't be soft, she thought as her gaze lingered on it. It would be hard, and the taste essentially male. She could lean just a bit closer and...

Laurel's eyes widened at the drift of her own thoughts. Beneath Matt's fingers, her pulse scrambled before she yanked her hand away. Good Lord, *what* had gotten into her? He'd tease her for months if he had any idea how close she'd come to making a fool of herself.

"We'd better go back in," she said coolly. "It's nearly time for dinner."

Matt had an urge to grab her and take the kiss she'd very nearly given him. And if he did that, he'd lose whatever inching progress he'd made. He'd wanted her for a long time—too long—and was shrewd enough to know she would have refused ordinary advances from the first. Matt had chosen the out-of-the-ordinary, finding it had its amusements.

Patience, Matt reminded himself, was a crucial element of success—but she deserved one, small dig for making him pound with desire and frustration.

"So soon?" His voice was mild, his expression ironic. "If Olivia had sent you out here with Cartier I doubt you'd have cut the tour so short."

"She'd never have sent me out here with Jerry," Laurel said before the meaning of her statement sank in.

"Ah." It was a sound designed to infuriate.

"Don't start on Jerry," Laurel snapped.

Matt gave her an innocent grin. "Was I?"

"He's a very nice man," she began, goaded. "He's well mannered and—and harmless."

Matt threw back his head and roared. "God save me from being labeled harmless."

Her eyes frosted and narrowed. "I'll tell you what you are," she said in a low, vibrating voice. "You're insufferable."

"Much better." Unable to resist, he stepped closer and gathered her hair in one hand. "I have no desire to be nice, well mannered or harmless."

She wished his fingers hadn't brushed her neck. They'd left an odd little trail of shivers. "You've gotten your wish," she said, not quite evenly. "You're annoying, rude and..."

"Dangerous?" he supplied, lowering his head so that their lips were only inches apart.

"Don't put words in my mouth, Bates." Why did she feel as though she were running the last leg of a very long race? Struggling to even her breathing, Laurel took a step back and found herself against the wall of the trellis. She would have sidestepped if he hadn't moved so quickly, blocking her.

"Retreating, Laurellie?" No, it wasn't just temper, he thought, watching the pulse hammer at the base of her throat. Not this time.

Something warm moved through her, like a lazy river. Her spine snapped straight. Her chin jutted up. "I don't have to retreat from you. It's bad enough that I have to tolerate you day after day at the *Herald,* but I'll be damned if I'll stand here and waste my *own* time. I'm going in," she finished on a near shout, "because I'm hungry."

Shoving him out of her way, Laurel stormed back toward the house. Matt stayed where he was a moment, looking after her—the swinging hair, the long, graceful strides, the simmering fury. That, he thought, was one hell of a woman. Making love to her would be a fascinating experience. He intended to have it, and her, very soon.

Chapter Two

Because she was still seething from the night before, Laurel decided to walk to the paper. A half an hour in the warm air, shifting her way through people, pausing by store windows, listening to snatches of casual conversation from other pedestrians would go a long way toward soothing her agitation. The city, like the plantation house outside it, was an old, consistent love. Laurel didn't consider it a contradiction that she could be drawn to the elegant timelessness of Promesse d'Amour and the bustling rush of downtown traffic. For as long as she could remember, she'd straddled both worlds, feeling equally at home in each. She was ambitious—she was romantic. Practicality and dreaminess were both a part of her nature, but she'd never minded the tug-of-war. At the moment, she felt more comfortable with the noise and hustle around her than with the memory of a twilight garden.

What had he been up to? she asked herself again, jamming her hands in her pockets. Laurel felt she knew Matt well enough to understand that he rarely did anything without an underlying purpose. He'd never touched her quite like that before. Scowling into a shop window, Laurel recalled that Matthew Bates had rarely touched her at all in an entire year. And last night . . . last night, Laurel remembered, there had been something almost casual about the way his fingers had brushed the back of her neck and skimmed over her wrist. *Almost* casual, she repeated. But there'd been nothing casual about her response to it.

Obviously, he had caught her off-balance—intentionally, Laurel added with a deeper scowl. What she'd felt hadn't been excitement or anticipation, but simply surprise. She was fully recovered now. The garden had been moody, romantic. She'd always been susceptible to moods, that was why she'd found herself telling him foolish things. And why, just for a minute, she'd wanted to feel what it would be like to be held against him.

Blossoms and sunsets. A woman might find the devil himself attractive in that kind of a setting. Temporarily. She'd pulled herself back before she'd done anything humiliating, Laurel reminded herself.

Then there was her grandmother. Laurel gritted her teeth and waited for the light to change. Normally, Olivia's outlandish remarks didn't bother her in the least, but she was going too far when she insinuated that Matthew Bates was exactly what her granddaughter needed.

Oh, he'd lapped that up, Laurel remembered, glaring straight ahead. He was easily as impossible as the old girl herself—without her charm, Laurel added loyally. She took a deep breath of the city—exhaust, humanity, heat. Right now, she appreciated it for what it was: genuine. She wasn't going to let an absurd incident in a fantasy world spoil her day. Determined to forget it, and the man who'd caused it, she started to step off the curb.

"Good morning, Laurellie."

Surprised, she nearly stumbled when a hand shot and grabbed her arm. Good God, wasn't there anywhere in New Orleans she could get away from him? Turning her head, she gave Matt a long, cool look. "Car break down?"

Haughtiness suited her, he mused, as well as temper did. "Nice day for a walk," he countered smoothly, keeping her arm as they started to cross the street. He wasn't fool enough to tell her he'd seen her start out on foot and had followed the impulse to go after her.

Laurel made a point of disengaging her arm when they reached the sidewalk. Why the hell hadn't she just gotten into her car as she would have any other morning? Short of making a scene on the street, she was stuck with him. When she gave him another glance, she caught the amused look in his eye that meant he'd read her thoughts perfectly. After rejecting the idea of knocking him over the head with her purse, Laurel gave him a cold smile.

"Well, Matthew, you seemed to enjoy yourself last night."

"I like your grandmother, she's beautiful," he said so simply, she stopped short. When her brows drew together, he smiled and ran a finger down her nose. "Isn't that allowed?"

With a shrug, Laurel began to walk again. How was she supposed to detest him when he was being sweet and sincere? Laurel made another stab at it. "You encourage her."

"She doesn't need any encouragement," he stated all too accurately. "But I like to anyway."

Laurel wasn't quite successful in smothering a laugh. The sidewalk was crowded enough to make it necessary for their arms to brush as they walked. "You don't seem to mind that she's setting you up as my..."

"Lover?" he suggested, with the annoying habit of finishing her thoughts. "I think Olivia, for all her, ah, liberated ideas, has something more permanent in mind. She threw in the house for good measure."

Stunned, Laurel gaped at him. He grinned, and her sense of the ridiculous took over. "You'd better be sure she tosses in some cash; it's the devil to maintain."

"I admit, it's tempting." He caught the ends of Laurel's hair in his fingers. "The . . . house," he said when her gaze lifted to his, "isn't something a man turns down lightly."

She slanted a look at him, one she'd never aimed in his direction before. Under the lashes, sultry, amused and irresistible. "Matthew," Laurel said in a soft drawl, "you'll put me in the position of considering Jerry more seriously."

Then, he thought as desire crawled into his stomach, I'd have to quietly kill him. "Olivia'd disown you."

Laurel laughed and, without thinking, linked her arm through his. "Ah, the choices a woman must make. My inheritance or my sensibilities. I guess it's just too bad for both of us that you're not my type."

Matt put his hand on the glass door of the Herald Building before Laurel could pull it open. "You put *me* in the position, Laurellie," he said quietly, "of having to change your mind."

She lifted a brow, not quite as sure of herself as she'd been a moment before. Why hadn't she noticed these rapid mood swings in him before? The truth was, she admitted, she'd dedicated herself to noticing as little about him as possible. From the first moment he'd walked into the city room, she had decided that was the safest course. Determined not to lose the upper hand this time, she smiled as she pushed through the door. "Not a chance, Bates."

Matt let her go, but his gaze followed her progress through the crowded lobby. If he hadn't already been attracted to her, her words would have forced his hand. He'd always liked going up against the odds. As far as he was concerned, Laurel had just issued the first challenge. With an odd sort of smile, he moved toward the bank of elevators.

Laurel's entire morning was involved interviewing the director of a highway research agency. A story on road repair and detour signs wasn't exactly loaded with fire and flash, she mused, but news was news. Her job was to assimilate the facts, however dry they might be, and report. With luck she could get the story under the fold on page two. Perhaps the afternoon would yield something with a bit more meat.

The hallways, rarely deserted, were quiet in the late morning lull. Other reporters returned from, or were on their way to, assignments, but most were already in the field or at their desks. Giving a perfunctory wave to a colleague hurrying by with an on-the-run lunch of a candy bar, she began to structure her lead paragraph. Preoccupied, she turned toward the city room and jolted another woman. The contents of the woman's purse scattered onto the floor.

"Damn!" Without glancing over, Laurel crouched down and began to gather things up. "Sorry, I wasn't looking where I was going."

"It's all right."

Laurel saw a very small hand reach out for a plain manila envelope. The hand was shaking badly. Concerned, she looked over at a pale blonde with pretty features and red-rimmed eyes. Her lips were trembling as badly as her hands.

"Did I hurt you?" Laurel took the hands in hers instinctively. A stray, an injured bird, a troubled stranger— she'd never been able to resist anything or anyone with a problem.

The woman opened her mouth, then closed it again to shake her head violently. The fingers Laurel gripped quivered helplessly. When the first tears rolled down the pale face, Laurel forgot the noise and demands of the city room, the notes scrawled in the book in her bag. Helping the woman up, Laurel led her through the maze of desks and into the glass-walled office of the city editor.

"Sit down," she ordered, nudging the blonde into a faded leather chair. "I'll get you some water." Without waiting for an agreement, Laurel strode out again. When she came back, she noted that the woman had swallowed her tears, but her face hadn't lost that wounded, bewildered expression. "Come on, sip this." After offering the paper cup, Laurel sat on the arm of the chair and waited.

Inside the office, she could hear the muted echo of activity from the city room. It was early enough in the day that desperation hadn't struck yet. Deadline panic was hours away. What desperation there was came from the blonde's efforts to steady her breathing. Hundreds of questions buzzed in Laurel's mind, but she gave the woman silence.

"I'm sorry." She crushed the now empty paper cup in her fingers before she looked up at Laurel. "I don't usually fall apart that way."

"It's all right." Laurel noticed the woman was slowly, systematically tearing the paper cup to shreds. "I'm Laurel Armand."

"Susan Fisher." Blankly, she looked down at the scraps of paper in her lap.

"Can I help, Susan?"

That almost started the tears again. Such simple words, Susan thought as she closed her eyes against them. Why should they make her feel all the more hopeless? "I don't know why I came here," she began jerkily. "I just couldn't think of anything else. The police . . ."

Laurel's reporter's drive rose to tangle with her protective instincts. Both were too natural to her for her to even notice them. She laid a hand on Susan's shoulder. "I work here; you can talk to me. Would you like to start at the beginning?''

Susan stared up at her. She no longer knew whom to trust, or if indeed trust was a word to believe in. This woman looked so confident, so sure of herself. She'd never had her life shattered. Why would this poised, vibrant-looking woman listen, or believe?

Susan's eyes were blue, soft and light and vulnerable. Laurel didn't know why they made her think of Matt, a man she thought had no sensitivity at all, yet they did. She put her hand over Susan's. "I'll help you if I can."

"My sister." The words tumbled out, then stopped with a jerk. With an effort, Susan swallowed and began again. "My sister, Anne, met Louis Trulane a year ago."

Louis? The name shot through Laurel's mind so that the hand over Susan's stiffened. Bittersweet memories, loyalties, growing pains. What could this tearful, frightened woman have to do with Louis? "Go on," Laurel managed, making her fingers relax.

"They were married less than a month after they met. Anne was so much in love. We had—we were sharing an apartment at the time, and all she could talk about was Louis, and moving here to live in the fabulous old house he owned. Heritage Oak. Do you know it?''

Laurel nodded, staring off into nothing more than her own memories. "Yes, I know it."

"She sent me pictures of it. I just couldn't imagine Anne living there, being mistress of it. Her letters were full of it, and of Louis, of course." Susan paused as her breath came out in a shudder. "She was so happy. They were already talking about starting a family. I'd finally made arrangements to take some time off. I was coming to visit her when I got Louis's letter."

Laurel turned to take Susan's hand in a firmer grip. "Susan, I know—"

"She was dead." The statement was flat and dull, with shock still lingering around the edges. "Anne was dead. Louis wrote—he wrote that she'd gone out alone, after dark, wandered into the swamp. A copperhead bite, he said. If they'd found her sooner... but it wasn't until the next morning, and it was too late." Susan pressed her lips together, telling herself she had to get beyond the tears. The time for them was over. "She was only twenty-one, and so lovely."

"Susan, it must've been dreadful for you to hear that way. It was a terrible accident."

"Murder," Susan said in a deadly calm voice. "It was murder."

Laurel stared at her for a full ten seconds. Her first inclination to soothe and comfort vanished, replaced by a whiff of doubt, a tingle of interest. "Anne Trulane died of a snakebite and exposure. Why do you call it murder?"

Susan rose and paced to the window. Laurel hadn't patted her hand, hadn't made inane comments. She was still listening, and Susan felt a faint flicker of hope. "I'll tell you what I told Louis, what I told the police." She took an extra moment to let the air go in and out of her lungs slowly. "Anne and I were very close. She was always gentle, sensitive. She had a childlike sweetness without being childish. I want you to understand that I knew Anne as well as I know myself."

Laurel thought of Curt and nodded. "I do."

Susan responded to this sign of acceptance with a sigh. "Ever since she was little, Anne had a phobia about dark places. If she had to go into a room at night, she'd reach in and hit the light switch first. It was more than just habit,

it was one of those small fears some of us never outgrow.
Do you know what I mean?''

Thinking of her own phobia, she nodded again. "Yes,
I know.''

Susan stepped away from the window. "As much as
Anne loved that house, having the swamp so near bothered her. She'd written me that it was like a dark closet—
something she avoided even in the daytime. She loved
Louis, wanted to please him, but she wouldn't go through
it with him.''

She whirled back to Laurel with eyes no longer calm, but
pleading. "You have to understand, she adored him, but
she wouldn't, couldn't do that for him. It was like an obsession. Anne believed it was haunted—she'd even worked
herself up to the point where she thought she saw lights out
there. Anne would never have gone in there alone, at
night.''

Laurel waited a moment, while facts and ideas raced
through her mind. "But she was found there.''

"Because someone took her.''

In silence, Laurel measured the woman who now stood
across from her. Gone was the defenseless look. Though
the eyes were still puffy and red-rimmed, there was a determination in them, and a demand to be believed. An
older sister's shock and loyalty perhaps, Laurel mused, but
she let bits and pieces of the story run through her mind,
along with what she knew of Anne Trulane's death.

It had never been clear why the young bride had wandered into the swamp alone. Though Laurel had grown up
with swamps and bayous, she knew they could be treach-
erous places, especially at night, for someone who didn't
know them. Insects, bogs...snakes.

She remembered too how Louis Trulane had closed out
the press after the tragedy—no interviews, no comment.

As soon as the inquest had been over, he'd retreated to Heritage Oak.

Laurel thought of Louis, then looked at Susan. Loyalties tugged. And pulling from both sides was a reporter's instinct she'd been born with. The whys in life always demanded an answer.

"Why did you come to the *Herald,* Susan?"

"I went to see Louis last night as soon as I got into town. He wouldn't listen to me. This morning I went to the police." She lifted her hands in a gesture of futility. "Case closed. Before I had a chance to think about it, I was here. Maybe I should hire a private investigator, but..." Trailing off, she shook her head. "Even if that were the right way to go, I don't have the money. I know the Trulanes are a powerful, respected family, but there has to be a way of getting at the truth. My sister was murdered." This time her voice quivered on the statement and the color that had risen to her cheeks from agitation faded.

Not as strong as she wants to be, Laurel realized as she rose. "Susan, would you trust me to look into this?"

Susan dragged a hand through her hair. She didn't want to fall apart now, not now when someone was offering the help she needed so badly. "I have to trust someone."

"There're a few things I have to do." Abruptly, Laurel became brisk. If there was a story, and she smelled one, she couldn't think of old ties, old memories. "There's a coffee machine in the lobby. Get a cup and wait for me there. When I've finished, we'll get something to eat—talk some more."

Asking no questions, Susan gathered up her purse, watching the torn bits of the paper cup drift to the floor. "Thank you."

"Don't thank me yet," Laurel advised. "I haven't done anything."

Susan paused at the door to glance over her shoulder. "Yes, you have."

Mouth pursed in thought, Laurel watched Susan wind her way through the desks in the city room. Anne Trulane, she thought, and let out a sigh. Louis. Good God, what kind of wasps' nest was she poking into?

Before she could formulate an answer, the city editor came in, his thin face creased into a scowl, his tired eyes annoyed. "Damn it, Laurel, this is a newspaper, not a Miss Lonelyhearts service. When one of your friends has a fight with her boyfriend, find someone else's office to flood. Now move it." He flopped down behind his cluttered desk. "You've got a story to write."

Laurel walked over to the desk and perched on the corner. Don Ballinger was her godfather, a man who had often bounced her on his knee. If it came to a toss-up between personal affection and news copy, the copy'd win hands down. Laurel expected no less. "That was Anne Trulane's sister," she said mildly when he opened his mouth to swear at her.

"Trulane," he repeated as his wispy brows drew together. "What'd she want?"

Laurel picked up a hunk of fool's gold Don used as a paperweight and shifted it from hand to hand. "To prove her sister was murdered."

He gave a short bark that might have been a laugh or a sound of derision. Don took a cigarette out of the desk drawer and ran it lovingly through his fingers. He stroked it, caressed it, but didn't light it. He hadn't lit one in sixteen days, ten hours...twenty-two minutes. "Snakebite," Don said simply, "and a night's exposure don't add up to murder. What about the story on the highway agency?"

"The sister tells me that Anne had a phobia about the dark," Laurel continued. "Anne supposedly mentioned the swamp where she died in her letters. She hadn't set foot in it, and didn't intend to."

"Obviously she changed her mind."

"Or someone changed it for her."

"Laurel—"

"Don, let me do some poking around." Laurel studied the glittering paperweight as she spoke. Things weren't always as they seemed, she mused. Not nearly always. "It couldn't hurt. If nothing else I could work up a human interest piece."

Don scowled down at his cigarette, running a finger from filter to tip. "Trulane won't like it."

"I can deal with Louis," she said with more confidence than she felt. "There's something in this, Don. There was never any clear reason why Anne Trulane went out there alone. She was already dressed for bed."

They both knew the rumors—that she'd been meeting a lover, that Louis had bracketed her to the house until she'd simply gone out blindly, then lost herself. Don put the cigarette in his mouth and gnawed on the filter. The Trulanes were always good copy. "Nose around," he said at length. "It's still fresh news." Before Laurel could be too pleased that she'd won the first round, he dropped the bomb. "Bates covered the story, work with him."

"Work with Bates?" she repeated. "I don't need him. It's my lead, my story."

"His beat," Don countered, "and no one's story until there is one."

"Damn it, Don, the man's insufferable. I'm not some junior reporter who needs a proctor, and—"

"And he has the contacts, the sources and knows the background." He rose while Laurel simmered. "We don't play personality games on the *Herald,* Laurel. You work together." After shooting her a last look, he stuck his head out the door. "Bates!"

"You can't play personality games with someone who has none," Laurel muttered. "I'm the one who knows the Trulanes. He'll just get in my way."

"Sulking always was a bad habit of yours," Don commented as he rounded his desk again.

"I am not sulking!" she protested as Matt sauntered into the room.

He took one look at Laurel's furious face, lifted a brow and grinned. "Problem?"

Laurel controlled the urge to hiss at him, and sank into a chair. With Matthew Bates around, there was always a problem.

"Cheer up," Matt advised a few minutes later. "Before this is over, you might learn something."

"I don't need to learn anything from you." Laurel swung toward the elevator.

"That," he murmured, enjoying the way her lips formed into a pout, "remains to be seen."

"You're not taking on an apprentice, Bates, but a partner." She jammed her fists into her pockets. "Don insisted on it because you'd covered the investigation and the inquest. You could make it easy on both of us by just giving me your notes."

"The last thing I do," Matt said mildly, "is give anyone my notes."

"And the last thing I need is to have you breathing down my neck on this. It's *my* story."

"That really stuck where it hurts, didn't it?" Casually, he pushed the button on the elevator, then turned to her.

"Didn't your papa ever tell you that sharing's good for the soul?"

Fuming, Laurel stepped into the car and pushed for lobby. "Go to hell."

She didn't know he could move quickly. Perhaps this was her first lesson. Before she had an inkling what he was doing, Matt punched a button and stopped the car between floors. Even as her mouth fell open in surprise, he had her backed up against the side wall. "Watch how far you push," he warned softly, "unless you're willing to take a few hard shoves yourself."

Her throat was so dry it hurt. She'd never seen his eyes frost over like this. It was frightening. Fascinating. Odd, she thought she'd convinced herself he didn't have a temper, but now that it was about to grab her by the throat, she wasn't surprised. No, it wasn't surprise that had the chill racing over her skin.

She was frightened, Matt observed. But she wasn't cringing. Common sense told him to back off now that his point had been made. But a year was a very long time. "I think I'll just get this out of my system now, before we get started."

He saw her eyes widen, stunned as he lowered his mouth toward hers. A twist of amusement curved his lips as he allowed them to hover a breath from hers. "Surprised, Laurellie?"

Why wasn't she moving? Her body simply wouldn't respond to the commands of her brain. She was almost certain she was telling her arms to push him away. Good God, he had beautiful eyes. Incredibly beautiful eyes. His breath whispered over her skin, trailing into her mouth through lips that had parted without her knowledge. He smelled of no more than soap—basic, simple. Wonderful.

In an effort to clear her senses, Laurel straightened against the wall. "Don't you dare—"

The words ended with a strangled sound of pleasure as his lips skimmed over hers. It wasn't a kiss. No one would consider such a thing a kiss: a breath of a touch without pressure. It was more of a hint—or a threat. Laurel wondered if someone had cut the cables on the elevator.

She didn't move, not a muscle. Her eyes were wide open, her mind wiped clean as he stepped fractionally closer so that his body made full contact with hers—firm, lean, strong. Even as her system jolted, she didn't move. His mouth was still whispering on hers, so subtly, so impossibly light she might have imagined it. When she felt the moist tip of his tongue trace her lips, then dip inside to touch, just touch, the tip of hers, the breath she'd been holding shuddered out.

It was that quiet, involuntary sound of surrender that nearly broke his control. If she'd spit and snarled at him, he could have dealt with it easily. He'd been angry enough to. He hadn't expected stunned submission, not from her. Over the anger came a tempting sense of power, then an ache—gnawing and sweet—of need. Even as he nipped his teeth into her soft bottom lip he wondered if he'd ever have her at quite such a disadvantage again.

God, he wanted to touch her, to slip that neat little blouse off her shoulders and let his hands mold slowly, very, very slowly, every inch of her. That skin of hers, pale as a magnolia, soft as rainwater, had driven him mad for months. He could have her now, Matt thought as he nibbled ever so gently at her lips. He was skilled enough, she off guard enough that he could take her there on the floor of the elevator before either of them had regained their senses. It would be crazy, wonderfully crazy. Even as she stood still, he could all but taste that passion fighting to overcome her surprise and reach out for him. But he had different plans for the seduction of Laurel Armand.

So he didn't touch her, but lazily backed away. Not once during those shivering two minutes had she taken her eyes off his. Laurel watched that clever, tortuous mouth curve as he again pressed the button for the lobby. The elevator started with a rumble and jerk.

"A pity we're pressed for time," Matt commented easily, then gave the elevator car a careless glance. "And space."

Layer by layer the mists that had covered her brain cleared until she could think with perfect clarity. Her eyes were glimmering green slits, her ivory skin flushed with rage as she let out a stream of curses in a fluid, effortless style he had to admire.

"Did you know you completely drop your *r*'s when your temper's loose?" Matt asked pleasantly. "It's an education in regional cadence. Truce, Laurel." He held up his hand, palm out as she drew breath to start again. "At least a professional one until we run down this lead. We can take up the private war when we're off duty."

She bit back a retort and smoldered as the elevator came gently to a stop. It wouldn't instill much confidence in Susan Fisher if the two of them were taking potshots at each other. "An armed truce, Bates," she compromised as they stepped into the lobby. "Try anything like that again, and you'll be missing some teeth."

Matt ran his tongue over them experimentally. "Sounds reasonable." He offered his hand, and though she didn't trust that sober expression on his face, Laurel accepted. "Looks like I buy you lunch after all."

Removing her hand, Laurel straightened the purse on her shoulder. "Big talk on an expense account."

Grinning, he swung a friendly arm around her as they moved toward the rear of the lobby. "Don't be cranky, Laurellie, it's our first date."

She snorted, and tossed her head—but she didn't push his arm away.

Chapter Three

Matt chose a noisy restaurant in the French Quarter because he always found it easier to make people talk if they weren't sure they could be heard. He'd sensed, from the introduction, that while Susan Fisher had given her trust to Laurel, she was withholding judgment on him. For the moment, he'd decided to let Laurel lead the way.

He was amiable, sympathetic, as he filed away Susan's every word and gesture. She was a woman, Matt decided, who had buckled under pressure and was fighting her way back up. She still had a long way to go, but on one point she wouldn't be swayed. She'd known her sister. Susan wasn't going to let Anne's death rest until all the facts were laid bare. Perhaps Matt admired her for it all the more because her hands weren't quite steady.

He glanced at Laurel and nearly smiled. She'll take in any stray, he mused, though he didn't doubt she'd bite his head off if he suggested it. She didn't want to be considered soft or vulnerable, particularly by him. They were colleagues or, more accurately, competitors. He'd always enjoyed going head to head with her, reporter to reporter. And after that two minutes between floors on the elevator, he didn't think she'd forget he was a man. He wasn't going to give her the chance to.

Pouring more coffee into Susan's cup, Matt sent Laurel a silent signal that it was his turn. Her slight shrug showed him that the truce was still on. "Your sister died nearly a month ago, Susan." He said it softly, watching her face. "Why did you wait so long before bringing all this up?"

She dropped her gaze to her plate, where she'd been pushing food around for twenty minutes. Over her head, Laurel's eyes met Matt's, brows raised. He could almost hear the question in them. *What the hell's this?* But she knew her job. He felt they were already partners without having stated the ground rules. I question. You soothe.

"Susan." Laurel touched her arm. "We want to help you."

"I know." Setting down her fork, she looked up again, skimming over Matt to settle on Laurel. "It's hard to admit it, but I didn't cope with Anne's death well. The truth is I just fell apart. I stopped answering my phone—didn't leave my apartment. Lost my job." She pressed her lips together. When she spoke again they had to strain to hear her over the cheerful din in the restaurant. "The worst is, I didn't even come down for the funeral. I suppose I was pretending it wasn't happening. I was the only family she had left, and I wasn't here."

"That isn't important. No, it's not," Laurel insisted when Susan began to speak. "You loved her. In the end love's all that really matters." Looking over, she saw Matt watching her steadily. For a moment, Laurel forgot Susan, suspicions, the noise and scents of the restaurant. She'd expected to see cynicism in his eyes, perhaps a very faint, very mocking smile. Instead, she saw understanding, and a question she didn't know how to answer. Without speaking, he lifted her hand to his lips, then set it down again.

Oh no, she thought, panicking. *Not him.* That wasn't just impossible, it was ludicrous. Dazed, she picked up her coffee, then set it back down when she saw her hand wasn't quite steady. That one long look had scattered her wits more effectively than the odd kiss that wasn't a kiss, on the elevator. As from a distance, she heard Susan's voice and forced herself to tune into it.

"It all hit me last week. I guess the first shock had passed and I started to think about her letters. It didn't fit." This time she looked up at Matt, demanding he understand. "Whenever she'd mention that swamp it was with a kind of loathing. If you'd understand just how much she hated the dark, you'd see that she would never have gone into the place alone, at night. Never. Someone took her there, Mr. Bates. Someone made her go."

"Why?" He leaned forward, and while his voice wasn't hard, it was direct. "Why would someone want to kill your sister?"

"I don't know." Her knuckles went white on the edge of the table as she fought the urge to just lay down her head and weep. "I just don't know."

"I covered the inquest." Taking out a cigarette, Matt reached for the pack of restaurant matches. He didn't want to be tough on her, but if she was going to fold it would be better if she did it now, before they got too deep. "Your sister'd been here less than a year and knew almost no one, as she and her husband rarely socialized. According to the servants, she doted on him, there was rarely a cross word between them. The basic motives for murder—jealousy, greed—don't apply. What else is there?"

"That doesn't matter." Susan turned back to Laurel again. "None of that matters."

"Let's take it a step at a time," Laurel suggested. "Do you still have your sister's letters?"

"Yes." Susan let out an unsteady breath. "Back at my hotel."

Matt crushed out his cigarette. "Let's go take a look at them."

When Susan was out of earshot, Laurel brushed close to Matt. "The shock may be over," she murmured, "but she's still not too sturdy. Matthew, I have a feeling about this."

"You've got too many feelings, Laurel."

She frowned at him as they skirted between tables. "Just what does that mean?"

"We have to deal with facts. If you want to play Girl Scout, you're going to cloud the issue."

"I should've known better," she said between her teeth. "For a minute back there I thought I saw some small spark of sensitivity."

He grinned. "I'm loaded with sensitivity. We can talk about it over drinks later."

"In a pig's eye." Laurel swung out the door behind Susan and made a point of ignoring Matt through the cab ride to the hotel.

It was seedy—the streets were narrow, the concrete chipped, the banisters peeling. Condensation gathered and dripped from the rusting balconies. The paint on the buildings was cracked and coated with layers of grime and moisture from the constant humidity. All the colors seemed to have faded into one—a steamy gray.

The alleyways were shadowed and dank. At night, Laurel knew, the street would be mean—the kind of street you avoided, or walked on quickly while glancing over your shoulder. From the open window across the street the sounds of an argument overpowered a scratchy jazz recording. A bony cat lay over the stoop and made a low, unfriendly sound in his throat when Susan opened the door.

When Laurel cautiously stepped around it, Susan offered an apologetic smile. "This place has its own... atmosphere."

Matt grinned as he cast a look around the dim lobby. "You should've seen the apartment where I grew up in New York."

The strained smile relaxed as Susan turned toward the stairs. "Well, it was here, and it was cheap."

Following them, Laurel frowned at Matt's back. She'd caught another glimpse of sensitivity. Odd. And, though she hated to admit it, the careless comment about his youth piqued her interest. Who had he been? How had he lived? She'd always been very careful not to allow herself to speculate.

The place was so quiet, so empty, that their footsteps echoed on the uncarpeted steps. Cracked paint and graffiti. Laurel studied Susan's profile as she unlocked the door. I'm going to get her out of here, she promised herself, by this afternoon. Catching the amused, knowing look Matt sent her, Laurel glared at him.

"After another merit badge, Laurellie?" he murmured.

"Shut up, Bates." While he chuckled, Laurel stepped into Susan's cramped, shadowy room. It had a narrow bed, a scarred dresser and no charm.

"That's funny, I know I left the shades up." Crossing the room, Susan jerked the cord so that the dusty white shade flapped up and the sun poured into the room. She flicked a switch that had a squeaky ceiling fan stirring the hot air. "I'll get the letters."

Laurel sat on the edge of the bed and looked up at Matt. "What part of New York did you come from?"

His brow lifted, as it did when he was amused—or evasive. "You wouldn't know it." His lips curved as he moved to sit beside her. "Ever been north of the Mason-Dixon line, Laurel?"

"I've been to New York several times," she began testily, then made a sound of frustration when his smile only widened. "Twice," she amended.

"The Empire State Building, Ellis Island, the U.N., tea at the Plaza and a Broadway show."

"You love being smug and superior, don't you?"

He ran a fingertip down her jaw. "Yeah."

She fought back a smile. "Did you know you become even more insufferable with prolonged contact?"

"Be careful," Matt warned. "I've a weakness for flattery."

With his eyes on her laughing ones, Matt lifted her hand, palm up, and pressed his lips to the center. He watched, pleased, when confusion replaced the humor in her eyes. Behind them, Susan began to pull out drawers frantically. They didn't notice.

"They're gone!" Susan swept a handful of clothes onto the floor and stared at the empty drawer. "They're gone, all of them."

"What?" A little dazed, Laurel turned to her. "What's gone?"

"The letters. All of Anne's letters."

Immediately Laurel was on her feet and sorting through Susan's jumbled clothing. "Maybe you put them somewhere else."

"No—there is nowhere else," she said with a dangerous edge of hysteria in her voice. "I put them all in this drawer. There were twelve of them."

"Susan." Matt's voice was cool enough to stiffen her spine. "Are you sure you brought them with you?"

She took long, deep breaths as her gaze shifted from Laurel to Matt. "I had every one of Anne's letters with me when I checked into this hotel. When I unpacked, I put them in that drawer. They were there when I dressed this morning."

Her hands weren't steady, Matt noticed, but her eyes were. He nodded. "I'll go check with the desk clerk."

As the door closed, Susan stared down at the crumpled blouse she held. "Someone was in this room," she said unsteadily. "I know it."

Laurel glanced at the shade Susan had lifted. "Are you missing anything else?"

"No." With a sigh, Susan let the blouse fall. "There isn't anything in here worth stealing. I suppose they realized that. It doesn't make any sense that they'd take Anne's letters."

"Matthew and I'll sort it out," Laurel told her, then was annoyed with herself for linking herself with Matt so easily. "In the meantime..." Bending, she began to gather Susan's clothes. "Can you type?"

Distracted, Susan stared at her. "Well, yes. I work—I worked," she corrected, "as a receptionist in a doctor's office."

"Good. Where's your suitcase?" she asked as she folded Susan's clothes on the bed.

"It's in the closet, but—"

"I have a place for you to stay, and a job—of sorts. Oh, this is lovely." She shook out the blouse Susan had crumpled.

"A job? I don't understand."

"My grandmother lives outside of town. Since my brother and I moved out, she's been lonely." The lie came out too easily to be questioned.

"But I couldn't just stay there."

"You'd pay for it." Laurel grinned as she turned back. "Grandma's been threatening to write her memoirs and I've just about run out of excuses for not typing them up for her. You won't be bored. She's eighty-two and didn't give up men until... Actually, she hasn't given them up at all. If I weren't so busy, I'd love to do it myself. As it is, you'd be doing me quite a favor."

"Why are you doing this for me?" Susan asked. "You don't know me."

"You're in trouble," Laurel said simply. "I can help."

"Just that easy?"

"Does help have to be complicated? Get your suitcase," Laurel ordered before Susan could work out an answer. "You can pack while I see what Matthew's come up with." As she slipped into the hall, Laurel bumped into him. She let the door click shut behind her. "Well?"

"The clerk didn't see anyone." Matt leaned against the wall and lit a cigarette. "But then he's more interested in cheating at solitaire in the back room than covering the desk." He blew out a stream of smoke that rose to the ceiling and hung there. "I spoke to the woman who does the rooms. She didn't pull the shades."

"Then someone was in there."

"Maybe."

Laurel ignored this and stared at the opposite wall. "Susan thinks it was just a break-in. In her state of mind that's all for the best."

"You're playing mama, Laurel."

"I am not." Angry, she looked back at him. "It'll be a lot easier to sort through this if she doesn't start thinking someone's deliberately trying to stop her."

"There's no reason for her to think that at this point," Matt said dampeningly. "What's she doing?"

"Packing," Laurel muttered.

He nodded. It wasn't wise for her to stay where she was. "Where's she going?"

Laurel angled her chin. "To my grandmother."

Not quite suppressing a smile, Matt studied the tip of his cigarette. "I see."

"You couldn't see through barbed wire. And don't start spouting off about my getting too personally involved, or—"

"All right." He crushed out the cigarette on the dusty, scarred floor. "And I won't comment that you're a very sweet, classy lady. I'll get a cab," he added when Laurel only stared at him.

Just when I think I understand him, she mused, he throws me a curve. If I'm not careful, Laurel added as his footsteps echoed off the stairs. If I'm not very, very careful, I'm going to start liking him. On that uncomfortable thought, she went back in to hurry Susan along.

In under ten minutes, Laurel was in the back of a cab with Matt, glancing behind her at the taxi that would take Susan to her grandmother.

"Stop worrying about her," Matt ordered. "Olivia'll keep her mind off her sister, and everything else."

With a shrug, Laurel turned back around. "I don't doubt that. But I'm beginning to doubt that Anne Trulane walked into that swamp alone."

"Let's stick with the facts. Motive." Absently, he wound a lock of Laurel's hair around his finger—a habit he'd recently developed and rather enjoyed. "There doesn't seem to be any. Women aren't lured into swamps for no reason."

"Then there was one."

"No sexual assault," Matt continued, half to himself. "She didn't have any money on her own—and her only heir would've been Susan in any case . . . or her husband. He has a sister, but I can't see any benefit there."

"The last people I'd consider as murder suspects would be Louis or Marion Trulane. And there are other motives for murder than sex and money."

He lifted a brow at her tone but continued to toy with her hair. "True, but those always spring to mind. Most of us are fond of both."

"Some think beyond your scope, Matthew. There's jealousy, if we go back to your two favorites. Louis is rich and attractive. Someone might have pictured herself in Anne's place."

He caught something—the drift of something he didn't quite understand. And didn't like. "Do you know him well?"

"Louis?" A smile touched her mouth, a gentle one. It reminded him that Laurel had never once looked at him that way. "As well as anyone, I suppose—or I did. He taught me to ride when I was a girl, let me tag along after him when I was ten and he was, oh, twenty-one or -two. He was a beautiful man—and very patient with a girl's infatuation."

When he discovered his fingers were no longer relaxed, Matt released the tendril of hair. "You got over it, I suppose."

Hearing the cynicism in his voice, Laurel turned, the half smile still on her face. "Weren't you ever in love, Matthew?"

The look he gave her was long and guarded while several uncomfortable emotions moved through him. Her eyes were soft; so was her mouth, her skin. If they'd been alone, he might not have answered the question at all, but would simply have taken what he found he needed so badly. "No," he said at length.

"It softens something in you, something that never quite goes away for that particular person." With a sigh, she sat back against the seat. It had been a long time since she'd let herself remember how sweet it had been, and how hurtful. She'd only been a child, and though her dreams had been fairy tales, she'd believed them. "Louis was very important to me. I wanted a knight, and I think he understood that well enough not to laugh at me. And when he married..." She lifted her hands and let them fall. "It broke my heart. Do you know about his first wife?"

Matt was staring down at the hands in her lap; small, elegant hands with the nails painted in the palest of corals and a smoky emerald in an intricate old setting on her finger. An heirloom, he thought. She would have heirlooms, and genteel ancestors—and memories of riding lessons from a tall young man, dashing enough to be a knight.

"Bits and pieces," Matt mumbled as the cab pulled to the curb. "Fill me in later."

Laurel climbed out of the cab, then meticulously brushed off her skirt. "That's perilously close to an order, Bates. Since Don didn't lay down any ground rules, maybe you and I should take care of that ourselves."

"Fine." He didn't know why he was angry. He studied her with eyes narrowed against the glare of the sun. "This is my beat."

With an effort, Laurel smothered the flare of temper. "And it's my lead."

"If you want to get anywhere with it," he said evenly, "you'll leave certain areas to me. When's the last time you fought your way through the red tape in there?" Matt jerked his head toward the station house beside them.

"I've untangled red tape before."

"Not in there," he countered before he took her arm.

"Just a minute, Bates." Laurel pushed his hand away and faced him. "The one thing you're going to understand, is that I may have no choice but to work with you on this story, but the operative word is *with,* not *for.* For the moment, however much it galls me, we're partners.''

This seemed to amuse him as the temper turned into an odd little smile. ''A nice ring to that. Partners,'' he agreed, taking her hand. ''It might become a habit.''

''The danger of that's slim to none. Would you stop touching me?''

''No,'' he said amiably as they climbed the steps.

Voices boomed off the walls of the station house. Disgruntled voices, insolent voices, irate voices. It smelled dankly, stalely of humanity. Sweat, coffee, cigarettes, alcohol. Five members of opposing street gangs leaned against a wall and eyed each other. A woman with a badly bruised face huddled in a chair and spoke in undertones to a harassed-looking officer who nodded and typed out her statement with two fingers. A young girl in snug shorts snapped her gum and looked bored.

He'd seen it all before—and more. After a cursory glance around, Matt moved through the people and desks. The officers, the victims, the accused, paid no more attention to him than he to them.

A slim brunette in a wilting uniform cupped a phone on her shoulder and lifted a hand in salute. Matt perched on the corner of her desk. Laurel stood beside him, watching as two elderly men nearly came to blows before they were pulled apart.

''Well, Matt, what brings you to paradise?'' The brunette set down the phone and smiled at him.

''How you doing, Sarge?''

The brunette tipped back in her chair to give him a long, thorough look. ''I haven't changed my phone number here—or at home.''

''The city keeps us both pretty tied up, doesn't it? Been to the Nugget lately?''

She picked up a pen and tapped it lightly against her mouth. "Not since last month. Want to buy me a drink?"

"You read my mind, but I have a little business."

Letting out a quick laugh, the sergeant dropped her pen onto a blotter crisscrossed with scrawled names and numbers. "Sure. What do you want, Matt?"

"A quick glimpse at the file on a case—a closed case," he added. "Need to do a little backtracking on a story I did, maybe a follow-up."

Her eyes narrowed. "What case?"

"Anne Trulane."

"Sensitive ground, Matt." Her eyes drifted past his to Laurel's.

"Laurel Armand, Sergeant Carolyn Baker. Laurel and I are on assignment together," Matt said smoothly. "She's an old family friend of the Trulanes. Thought maybe we'd do something a little more in depth. Case is closed, Sarge, and hell, I covered the thing from start to finish."

"You've already seen the report."

"Then it can't hurt for me to see it again." He gave her a charming smile. "You know I play it straight, Carolyn, no printing privileged information, no hints in a story that messes up an investigation."

"Yeah, you play it straight, Matt." She shot him a look that Laurel thought had more to do with personal feelings than professional ones, then shrugged. "It was all public knowledge at the inquest." Rising, she walked away to disappear into a side room. Beside them, the two old men hurled insults at each other.

"You always work that way, Matthew?"

Matt turned to give Laurel a bland smile. "What way?" When she remained silent and staring, he grinned. "Jealous, love? You've got my heart in your hand."

"I'd rather have it under my foot."

"Vicious," he murmured, then pushed off the desk when Carolyn came back in.

"You can look at the file, take it in the first holding room. It's empty." She gave a quick glance around at the cramped room. "For now," she added dryly. Opening a book, she turned it to face him. "Sign for it."

"I owe you one, Sarge."

She waited until he'd scrawled his signature. "I'll collect."

Chuckling, Matt turned to work his way through to the holding room. An interesting woman, Sergeant Baker. Strange that it was never she who crept into his mind at odd moments. Not her, nor any of the other...interesting women he knew. Just one woman.

"Have a seat," Matt invited, closing the door and shutting out most of the din. The chair he chose scraped over the floor as he pulled it away from a long, battered table.

"Cheerful place," Laurel muttered, glancing around at the dull white walls and dingy linoleum.

"Stick with City Hall if you want tidy offices and white collars." Opening the file, he began to scan it briskly.

He fits here, Laurel realized with a grudging kind of respect. For all his easygoing manner, there was a hard, tough edge underneath she'd only glimpsed briefly. The man on the elevator. Yes, she mused, he'd shown her that ruthless, searing temper there. And more. Laurel didn't want to think of that just yet.

But there was no getting around the fact that there were more facets to him than she'd wanted to believe. It was safer to consider him a shallow, inconsequential man who just happened to be a hell of a reporter. Seeing him now, completely at ease in the grim little room, made her wonder just how much he'd seen, how much he'd experienced. He dealt with the troubles, the griefs, the viciousness of people day after day, yet he didn't seem hard or cold, or overwhelmed by it. What made Matthew Bates tick? she wondered. And what made her suddenly so sure she had to find out?

"Nothing much here," he muttered, skimming the papers. "Autopsy report...no sexual abuse, contusions, lacerations attributed to her wandering through the swamp. Copperhead got her on the left calf. Cause of death snakebite, complicated by exposure. Time of death between 12:00 and 4:00 A.M." He handed the sheet to Laurel before going on to the investigator's report.

"Trulane was working late in his study. According to him, he thought his wife was upstairs in bed. He went up around two, found the bed empty. He searched the house, then woke his sister and the staff, searched the house again and the grounds."

Absently, he reached for a cigarette, found the pack empty and swore without heat. "None of her clothes were missing, all the cars were there. His call to the station came through at 2:57 A.M." He glanced over at Laurel. "Nearly an hour."

Her fingers were a bit damp on the autopsy report. "It's a big house. A sensible person doesn't call the police until he's sure he needs them."

After a slow nod, Matt looked back down at the report. "The police arrived at 3:15. The house was searched again, the staff questioned..." He mumbled for a moment, skimming the words. "Anne Trulane's body was found at approximately 6:00 A.M., in the southeast section of the swamp."

He'd been there. Matt remembered the gray light, the hot, humid smells, the nasty feel of the swamp even before they'd come across death.

"No one could account for her being out there. According to Marion Trulane, the sister-in-law, Anne had a phobia about the place. That fits with Susan's claim," he murmured. "Trulane stuck with his story about working late, and wouldn't elaborate."

"Have you ever found your wife dead?" Laurel demanded as she took the report from Matt. "It's just possible that he was upset."

He let the scathing words slip off him. "The conclusion is she felt compelled to go in—maybe to face her fears, got lost, bitten, and wandered around until she lost consciousness." He glanced over at Laurel. Her brows were drawn together as she read the report for herself. "You still buddies enough to get us into the house, ask some questions?"

"Hmm? Oh, yes, I suppose so. They'll talk to me. You too," she added, "if you spread some of your charm around."

His mouth twisted into a grin. "I didn't think you'd noticed."

"I noticed that you can pull it out rather successfully when you put your mind to it. It's a bit deliberate for my tastes, but effective enough."

"Please, Laurellie, compliments are so embarrassing."

Ignoring him, Laurel set the investigator's report aside. "Louis hasn't had an easy time. He's closed himself in since his first marriage failed, but I think he'll talk to me."

Idly, Matt twisted the empty pack of cigarettes into a mass of foil and cellophane. "His wife ran off with his brother?"

"It was horrible for Louis." She slipped the next paper from the file as Matt gazed up at the ceiling, lost in thought.

Her skin went to ice, her stomach knotted, but she couldn't look away. The police photo was black and white and grim. She'd seen death before, but not like this. Never like this. Appalled, transfixed, she stared down at Anne Fisher Trulane. Or what she had come to.

Oh God, Laurel thought as her head went light and her stomach rolled. It's not real. It's a gruesome joke. Just someone's twisted idea of a joke.

"How long ago did—" Matt broke off as he shifted his gaze to Laurel. Her skin was dead white, her eyes full of horror. Even as he swore, he whipped the photo away from her, then pushed her head down between her knees. "Breathe deep," he ordered sharply, but his hand was abruptly gentle on the back of her head. Hearing her breath shudder in and out, he cursed himself more savagely. What the hell had he been thinking of? "Easy, love," he murmured, kneading the tension at the base of her neck.

"I'm all right." But she wasn't so sure. Laurel took an extra moment before she tried to straighten in the chair. When Matt's arms came around her, she let her head rest on his shoulder. "I'm sorry, that was stupid."

"No." He tilted her head back. "I'm sorry." Very slowly, very carefully, he brushed the hair away from her face.

She swallowed, hard. "I guess you're used to it."

"God, I hope not." He drew her close again so that her face was pressed against his neck.

She felt safe there. The chill was passing. Laurel relaxed, letting him stroke her hair, allowing the warm, real scent of him to block out the institutional smell of the waiting room. She could feel the steady beat of his heart against her. Life. When his lips brushed her ear, she didn't move. It was comfort he offered and comfort she felt. She told herself that was all, as she held onto him as if she'd just discovered him.

"Matthew..."

"Hmmm?"

"Don't be too nice to me."

With her eyes closed, her face buried at his throat, she felt the smile. "Why not?"

"Just don't." A bit more steady, she drew away because it was much too easy to stay.

He cupped her face in his hand. "You're beautiful," he murmured. "Have I told you that before?"

Cautiously she moved out of reach. Treat it light, she warned herself. And think about it later. "No." She smiled and rose. "I always jot things like that down."

"Beautiful," he repeated. "Even if your chin is just a bit pointed."

"It is not." Automatically, she tilted it.

"Especially from that angle."

"I have very delicate features," Laurel told him decisively as she picked up her purse. No, damn it, her fingers were not steady yet. God, she had to get out of this place, get out and breathe again.

With his back to her, Matt slipped the photo back in the file folder, closing the cover before he turned around. "Except for the chin," he agreed, putting an arm around her shoulders as he started for the door.

With her hand on the knob, Laurel stopped and looked up at him. Her eyes were dark and more aware than they'd been before they'd come into that room. "Matthew." She leaned against him for a moment, just for a moment. "No one deserves to die that way."

He tightened his grip on her for a moment, just for a moment. "No."

Chapter Four

The bar was dim and cool. It was too early for the evening rush, too late for the afternoon regulars. With his mind still on Anne Trulane's file, Matt steered Laurel inside. No, no one deserved to die that way, but then life, and death, didn't always play according to the rules. He'd learned to accept that a long time ago.

Matt had been as quiet as Laurel since they'd walked out of the station house. He was thinking, analyzing. Remembering.

The phone had rung in the early hours of the morning—his source at the station house tipping him on Anne Trulane's disappearance. He'd arrived at Heritage Oak moments after the police. There'd been a mist, he recalled, thinner and nastier than a rain, and an air of silence. He'd sensed Louis Trulane hadn't wanted to call the outside for help. His answers had been clipped, his expression remote. No, he hadn't looked like a harried, concerned husband, but like a man who'd had his evening interrupted.

His sister, and the enclave of servants, had gathered around him a few paces back, in a move that had seemed like a defense before the search had spread into the marsh. It was a winding, humid place with shadows and small, secret sounds. Matt had felt a distaste for it without knowing why. He'd only known he'd rather have been searching the streets and alleyways than that steamy, dripping maze of shadow and bog.

They'd found her, too late, curled on the ground near a sluggish stream when dawn was just breaking. Mist, gray light, wet pungent smells. He'd heard a bird, a lark perhaps, calling in the distance. And he'd heard the crows. Matt remembered Louis Trulane's reaction. He'd been pale, cold and silent. If there'd been anger, grief or despair, he'd closed it inside. His sister had fainted, the servants had wept, but he'd simply stood....

"I'm going to call Louis."

"What?" Matt glanced over to find Laurel watching him.

"I'm going to call Louis, ask if he'll see us."

Slowly, he tore the wrapper from a fresh pack of cigarettes. "All right." He looked after her as she weaved her way through tables to the pay phone in the corner. It wasn't easy for her, Matt thought, and struck a match with more force than necessary. She was too close, too open. Whatever childhood feelings she'd had for Louis Trulane were still too important to her to allow her to see him objectively.

What about you, Bates? he asked himself as he blew out a stream of smoke. You detest him because of the way Laurel says his name. It was time, he told himself, that they both remembered their priorities. The story came first. It had to. If Laurel's relationship with the Trulanes got them in, so much the better. He'd been in the game too long to be under any illusions. People like the Trulanes could toss obstacles in a reporter's way until getting through them was like walking through a mine field.

Not that it would stop him from getting the story—it would only add to the time and the legwork. Either way, Matt mused, either way he was going to poke some holes into that sanctified wall the Trulanes had around themselves and their name.

He saw Laurel coming back, the sadness lingering in her eyes, the color only a hint in her cheeks. She'd get over it, he told himself as something seemed to tear inside him. Because she had to. He waited until she slid into the booth across from him.

"Well?"

"He'll see us at ten tomorrow."

Matt crushed out his cigarette, warning himself not to touch her. "You don't sound too thrilled about it."

"I used the pressure of an old friendship." She looked up then, meeting his eyes with a kind of weary defiance. "I hated it."

"You've got a job to do," he muttered, and found he'd reached for her hand before he could stop himself.

"I know. I haven't forgotten." Instinctively she tightened her fingers on his. "I don't have to like it to do it well." She knew she'd never be able to back off now, not after seeing that picture—not after imagining what Susan Fisher would have felt if she had seen it.

When the waitress stopped beside her, Laurel glanced up. She had to dull the image. Maybe it was weak, but she had to. "Martini," she said on impulse. "A dry martini with an illusion of vermouth."

"Two," Matt ordered, sending Laurel an off-center smile. "It only helps temporarily, Laurellie."

"That's good enough for now." Resting her elbows on the table, she leaned forward. "Matthew, I'm going to consume great quantities of alcohol. This is totally preplanned and I offer no excuses. I will promise, however, not to get sloppy. Naturally, I'll regret this tomorrow, but I think it'll be a lesson well learned."

He nodded, grinning because he saw she needed it. "Since I'm joining you, I'll try to maintain your high standards. In any case..." He leaned a bit closer. "I've often wondered what it would be like to get you drunk and have my way with you."

She laughed for the first time in hours. "There isn't enough gin in this place for that, Matthew."

"We'll see how you feel in a couple hours." Leaning back, he lit another cigarette. "Why don't you tell me about the Trulanes?"

"What about them?"

"Everything."

She sighed, then, picking up the glass the waitress set in front of her, sipped. "This might just be the only thing in New Orleans completely lacking in humidity."

Matt acknowledged this by tapping the rim of his glass against hers. "The Trulanes, Laurellie."

"All right—and don't call me that. Ancient history first," she began. "Heritage Oak was built in the early nineteenth century. The plantation was vast and rich. The Trulanes still own more land than anyone else in this part of Louisiana. Besides cotton and cattle, they were ship builders. The profits from that kept the plantation alive after the war. As far back as anyone would remember, the Trulanes've been an important part of New Orleans, socially, financially and politically. I'm sure Grandma has a large repertoire of stories."

"Undoubtedly," Matt agreed. "Let's just speed up the passage of time a bit. Something in this century."

"Just laying the groundwork." Laurel took a sip from her glass, then toyed with the stem. "Beauregard Trulane—"

"Come on."

"There's always a Beauregard," she said loftily. "Inherited Heritage Oak right after his marriage. He had three children: Marion, Louis and Charles." Her eyes smiled over the rim of her glass. "He was an enormous man, bellowing, dramatic. Grandma loved him. In fact, I've sometimes wondered... well." She grinned and shrugged. "His wife was beautiful, a very quiet, serene sort of woman. Marion looks a great deal like her. Aunt Ellen—I called her that—died less than six months after my mother. I was around six... I've always mixed them a bit in my mind."

With a shrug, she emptied her glass, not noticing that Matt signaled for another round. "In any case, after she died, old Beau went into a steady decline. Louis began to take over the business. Really, he was too young to face those kinds of pressures, but there wasn't much choice. He would've been about eighteen or nineteen at the time, and I suppose I already worshiped him. To me, he was a cross between Prince Charming and Robin Hood. He was kind to me, always laughing and full of fun. That's how I like to remember him," she murmured, and stared into her fresh drink.

"Things change," Matt said briefly. How did a man compete with a childhood memory? he asked himself, frustrated by the look on Laurel's face. Damned if he would. "You're not a child anymore, Laurel."

She shifted her gaze to his and held it steady. "No, but a good deal of my perspective on Louis is that of a child."

He inclined his head and told himself to relax. "Tell me about Marion."

"She's a couple years older than Louis, and as I said, has her mother's looks. When I was young I thought of her as my personal fairy godmother. She was always so poised, and so beautiful."

A picture of dark elegance and flawless skin ran through his mind. "Yes, I noticed."

"She's too old for you," Laurel said without thinking, then looked over with a frown when Matt burst out laughing. "Shut up, Bates, and let me finish."

"I beg your pardon," he said with his tongue in his cheek.

"Marion used to have me over," Laurel continued, rashly finishing off her second martini. "She'd give me tea and cakes in the parlor. She knew I adored Louis and used to tell me to hurry and grow up so Louis could marry me. I adored her too."

"She never married?"

"No. Grandma said she was too choosy, but I think she had a love affair that didn't work out. Once I was there on a gray, gloomy day and she told me if a woman had one great love in her life, it was enough. Of course, at the time I thought she was talking about Louis and me, but when I got older and remembered how she'd looked..." On a sigh, Laurel reached for her glass. "Women like Marion are easily hurt."

He looked at her, the soft skin, soft mouth, soft eyes. "Is that so?"

"Charles was different." Shaking off the mood, Laurel leaned back with her drink. "I suppose he was a bit like Curt, and I thought of him as an extra brother. He was dreamy and abstracted. He was going to be an artist, and when he wasn't sketching, he was studying or hanging around Jackson Square. They'd hung some of his paintings in the main hall—until he left."

"With the first Mrs. Trulane," Matt finished.

"Yes, twelve years ago. It was a nasty scandal, the sort that causes a lot of pain and fabulous headlines." She shook her head over the opposing loyalties and sighed. The martinis were taking the edge off. "Grandma could tell you a great deal more, but from what I remember, Louis came back from a business trip to find Elise and Charles gone. The rumor that buzzed from servants' wing to servants' wing was that there was a note. Most of their clothes and all of Charles's painting gear were gone."

Laurel looked beyond him, unaware that the bar was filling up with people and noise. Someone was playing on the piano in the rear. "That's when Louis changed. He closed himself off from everyone. The few times I did see him, all the laughter was gone. As far as I know, he's never heard from Charles or Elise. About four years ago, he finally filed for divorce. Marion told me he'd done it strictly as a legality, that he was bitter, very bitter. She worried about him. His second marriage was a surprise to everyone."

Idly, she watched the smoke from Matt's cigarette curl toward the ceiling. The fans spun gently, slicing at the smoke, stirring the air. He hadn't spoken in some time, but she didn't realize it was the quality of his listening that made it so easy to speak. "I called him, first because I really hoped he was happy, and second, because Louis Trulane's remarriage meant a good story. He sounded almost like his old self—older, certainly, but some of the spark was back. He wouldn't give me an interview, he said..." She frowned as she searched back for his words. "He said he'd married a child and he needed to keep spring to himself for a little while."

God, did she know what she did to him when her eyes took on that vulnerable, young look? He wanted to take her away somewhere, anywhere, so that nothing could hurt her. And if he tried, she'd think he was out of his mind. Matt crushed out his cigarette with deliberate care. "What do you know about the first Mrs. Trulane?"

"Nothing really." Looking up again, she smiled wryly. "Except I was horribly jealous of her. She was lovely in that soft, kind of misty style that no one can emulate. I do remember the wedding—pink and white magnolias, a huge, frothy wedding cake and beautiful dresses. Elise wore silk and lace with miles of train. She looked like a porcelain doll—gold and white and tiny. She looked like..." She trailed off, eyes wide, with her glass halfway to her lips. "Oh God, she looked like—"

"Like the second Mrs. Trulane," Matt finished. Leaning back, he signaled the waitress again. "Well, well."

"It doesn't mean anything," she began in a rush. "Only that Louis was attracted to a certain type of woman. The resemblance to his first wife doesn't add up to a motive for murder."

"It's the closest we've got. And we're still a long way from being certain Anne Trulane was murdered." Matt lifted a brow as he studied Laurel's face. "You're quick to rush to his defense, Laurellie. It's going to be difficult for you to think clearly if you don't let go of your childhood infatuation."

"That's ridiculous."

"Is it?" His lips curved without humor.

"Listen, Bates, I always think clearly, and whatever my feelings for Louis, they won't interfere with my work." She looked down at her empty glass. "I finished my drink."

"So I see." This time the amusement leaked through. Indignation was one of her most appealing expressions. She'd had enough of the Trulanes for the day, Matt decided. So had he. Unobtrusively, the waitress replaced empty glasses with fresh ones. "Well, that's for tomorrow. Why don't you bring me up to date on our favorite city councilman? I'm keeping a scrapbook."

"Why don't you leave Jerry alone?" Laurel demanded, starting on the next drink.

"Everyone's entitled to a hobby."

"Don't be so smug and superior," she mumbled into her glass. "Jerry's a very—very..."

"Pompous ass?" Matt suggested blandly, then grinned when she burst into a fit of giggles.

"Damn you, Matthew, if my brain weren't numb, I'd have thought of something." Blowing the hair out of her eyes, she set down her drink and folded her hands. "I find your continually rude comments on Jerry's personality annoying."

"Because I'm right?"

"Yes. I really hate it when you're right."

He grinned, then, tossing a few bills on the table, rose. "I'll walk you home, Laurel. Let's hope the fresh air doesn't clear your brain—you might just be receptive to a few of my baser instincts."

"It'd take more than three martinis to do that." She stood, letting out a long breath when the floor tilted gently under her feet.

"Four," he murmured as he took her arm. "But who's counting?"

"I'm only holding on to you because I have to," Laurel told him as they stepped outside. "After a couple blocks, I'll get my rhythm back."

"Just let me know when you want to go solo."

"How many did you have?"

"The same as you."

Laurel tilted her head back to study him and found the martinis spun not too unpleasantly in her head. "Well, you're taller, and heavier," she added with a smirk. "I have a very delicate build."

"So I've noticed."

She lifted a brow as they passed a sidewalk trumpeter. The sound of jazz was mellow and sad. "Have you really?"

"You could say I've made a study of it—journalistically speaking."

"What's that supposed to mean?"

He paused long enough to touch his lips to hers. "Don't press your luck."

"You have a funny way of kissing," she muttered as her head tilted onto his shoulder. "I don't know if I like it."

To his credit, Matt didn't slip a hand around her throat and squeeze. "We can have a debate on that subject later."

"I really thought you'd have a different technique," she went on. "You know, more . . . aggressive."

"Been spending time thinking about my technique?" he countered.

"I've given it some thought—journalistically speaking."

"It'd be safer to table this discussion until you can walk a straight line." He turned into the courtyard of the building they shared.

"You know, Matthew . . ." Laurel gripped the banister as they climbed the stairs. The steps weren't as steady as they'd been that morning. "You're not really so bad after three martinis."

"Four," he mumbled.

"Don't nitpick now that I've decided to tolerate you." Unzipping her purse, she began to fish for her keys. "Here, hold this."

Matt found himself holding a wallet, compact, notebook, broken earrings and several ticket stubs. "Anything else?" he said dryly.

"No, here they are—they always sink to the bottom."

Unceremoniously, he dumped the contents back in her purse and took the keys from her. "Are you going to let me in?" A pot of coffee, he mused as she leaned back against the door. A couple of aspirins and a dark room. He wasn't at all certain she could manage any of the three by herself. "We've been neighbors for nearly a year and I haven't had an invitation."

"What appalling manners." Giving him a misty smile, Laurel gestured him inside.

The room, like the woman, had soft edges, elegance and wit. There was the scent of potpourri with a touch of lavender. The colors were creams and roses. Lace at the curtains, velvet on the sofa. On the wall above a gleaming tea cart was a framed burlesque poster from the 1890s.

"It suits you."

"Really?" Laurel glanced around, unaccountably pleased with herself. "'S funny, even if I'd seen your place I wouldn't know if it suited you." Laurel dragged a hand through her hair as she tried to focus on him. She held it there as she swayed, only a little. "I don't really understand you at all. Framed newsprints or Picassos. In an odd sort of way, you're a fascinating man."

She was smiling at him, only an arm's length away. At the moment, Matt wasn't certain if she was being deliberately provocative or if the martinis were doing it for her. Either way, it wasn't any easier on him. He didn't have many rules, but one of them dealt strictly with making a move on a woman who might not remember it the next morning.

"Coffee," he said briefly and took her arm.

"Oh, did you want some?"

"You do," he said between clenched teeth. "Black."

"Okay." In the kitchen, she stared at the automatic coffee maker, brows knit. She'd have sworn she knew what to do with it.

"I'll make it," Matt told her, grinning again. "Can you handle the cups?"

"Certainly." Laurel rummaged in a cupboard, and though she rattled them dangerously, managed to set violet-trimmed china cups in their saucers on the counter. "I don't have any *beignets*."

"Coffee's fine."

"Guess if you *really* wanted some I could make 'em."

"I'll take a rain check."

"You're a good sport, Matthew." Laughing, she turned and tumbled into his arms. With a smile, she curled her arms around his neck. "You've got fabulous eyes," she said on a sigh. "I bet just everyone tells you that."

"Constantly." He put his hands on her waist, intending to draw her away. Somehow, she was pressed against him with his fingers spread over the thin material of her blouse. Desire curled inside him like a fist. "Laurel..."

"Maybe you should kiss me again, so I can figure out why I always think I don't want you to."

"Tomorrow," he murmured as he lowered his mouth toward hers, "if you remember, you're going to hate yourself for saying that."

"Mmmm, I know." Her lashes lowered as his lips brushed over hers. "That's not a kiss." She drew a long sigh as her nerve ends began to tingle. "It's fabulous." Her fingers crept into his hair to tangle and explore. "More..."

The hell with rules, Matt thought savagely. If he had to pay for what he took now, then he'd pay. And by God, it would be worth it. On an oath, he dragged her against him and crushed her mouth with his.

Instant fire. It flared from her into him—or him into her. The source didn't matter, only the results. She moaned. The sound had nothing to do with pain or with wonder, and everything to do with raw desire. Her body strained into his with a certainty. This is right, this had always been right. She found his tongue with hers and let passion and intimacy merge blindingly, then struggled for more.

At that moment, with her head spinning and her body humming, it no longer mattered that it should be he who touched off all the sparks, all the secrets raging in her. No one else ever had. No one else ever could. Again, above all the whirling thoughts in her mind was one simple demand: more.

He was losing. Perhaps he'd been losing since he'd first seen that face. Bits and pieces of himself were being absorbed and he no longer cared. She could have whatever she wanted as long as he could have her like this. Heated, melting, hungry.

Her taste wasn't delicate like her looks, but wild and daring. Her scent was airy, romantic, her mouth ripe with passion. Though he could feel her breasts yield against him, her hands demanded and took. Muttering threats, promises, pleas, he pressed his mouth to her throat and began to please himself.

Her pulse hammered. He could feel it beneath his lips, strong, fast. With a nip of his teeth it scrambled and raced to war with the low sound she made. Then his hands were on her, hard, rushing, urgent until the sound became his name. There was nothing casual about him now, not a trace of the easygoing, faintly amused man who sat across from her day after day. There was the aggression he'd carefully glossed over. The ruthlessness. The excitement.

He wanted her—too much for comfort. Too much for sanity. Perhaps she was all he'd ever wanted, the silkiness, the fire. When she was pressed against him like this, there was no past, no future, only now. Now was enough for a lifetime.

How could her mind be so clouded and her body so alive? Laurel thought she could feel her own blood racing through her veins. Is this what she'd been waiting for? This mindless freedom? It was enough—it was more than she'd ever dreamed of, more than she'd ever understood. She was far from understanding now, but her body was so busy controlling her mind, she didn't care. With a sound of possession and the strength of greed, she dragged Matt's mouth back to hers. It seemed as though her legs dissolved from the knees down.

She heard him swear against her mouth before he clutched her closer. Then he drew her away while she gripped his shoulders in protest, and for support. "Matthew..."

"The door." His voice wasn't any more steady than the rest of him. No, he wasn't steady, Matt realized as he held Laurel away from him. And maybe not quite sane. "Someone's at the door, Laurel. You'd better answer it."

"The door? Whose door?" She stared up at him, aroused, dazed.

"Your door." A faint smile touched his lips.

"Oh." She looked around the sun-washed kitchen as though she'd never seen it before. "I should answer it?"

He nearly dragged her back. Her flushed, bemused expression had his fingers tightening convulsively on her arms. Carefully, he released her. "Yeah." Disoriented, Laurel walked away. He'd come too close, Matt thought, too damn close to yanking her to the kitchen floor and taking her like a maniac. He turned to the hissing coffee-pot, not sure whether to be grateful to whoever was banging on the door, or to murder them.

Laurel felt as though she'd been swimming underwater and had come up much too quickly. Drunk? She pressed her fingers to her temple as she reached for the doorknob. Whatever the martinis had started, Matt had finished. She shook her head, hard, and when it didn't clear, gave up and opened the door.

"Laurel, you took so long answering I nearly went away." Jerry Cartier, three-piece-suited and vaguely annoyed, stared at her.

"Oh." Her blood was cooling, but the alcohol still swam in her head. "Hello, Jerry."

Because she stepped back, swinging the door wider, he came in. "What were you up to?"

"Up to?" she repeated... and remembered. Laurel let out a long breath. "Coffee," she murmured. "I was making coffee."

"You drink too much coffee, Laurel." He turned as she closed the door and leaned back on it. "It isn't good for your nerves."

"No." She thought of Matt. She hadn't realized she had so many nerves until a few moments ago. "No, you're probably right about that." She straightened as it occurred to her what Jerry would have to say if he realized just what she'd been drinking, and how much. The last thing she wanted was a twenty-minute lecture on the evils of alcohol. "Sit down, Jerry," she invited, thinking just how much she wanted to lie down—in a dark room—in silence. If she were lucky, very lucky, she could cross the room and get to the sofa without weaving. She took one hesitant step.

"You're not ready."

Laurel stopped dead. He was right, of course, but crawling wasn't such a good idea. Neither was standing still. "Ready?"

"For dinner," Jerry told her as his brows drew together."

"Hello, Jerry." Carrying a tray of steaming coffee and cups, Matt strolled in.

Jerry crossed one leg over the other. "Matthew."

After setting down the tray, Matt walked casually to where Laurel still stood. "Condemn any good buildings lately?" In an unobtrusive move, he took Laurel's arm and led her to the couch. As she sank down, she shot him a grateful look.

"That's not my jurisdiction," Jerry stated, lacing his fingers together. "The mayor did tell me just the other day about a building on the other side of town. Appalling plumbing."

"Is that so?"

"Coffee?" Laurel interrupted. Martinis or not, she couldn't sit there and let Matt calmly execute an unarmed man. Besides, if she didn't have some coffee, she was going to quietly lay her head on the arm of the sofa and doze off.

"Only a half cup," Jerry told her. "Are you sure you should have any more?"

She made a grab for the handle of the pot and prayed she could pour it. "I haven't had any for hours."

"So, how was your day, Jerry?" Matt asked him as he closed his hand over Laurel's on the handle. Hearing her small sigh of relief, he nearly grinned.

"Busy, busy. There never seems to be enough hours to get everything done."

Matt's gaze slid down to Laurel's, brushing over her mouth. "No, there doesn't."

Jerry reached for the cup Laurel passed him and had to lean to the right when she missed his hand. "Laurel," he began, giving her an oddly intent look. "Have you been—drinking?"

"Drinking?" She set her heel down hard on Matt's foot when he chuckled. "Jerry, I just poured." Lifting the cup to her lips, she drank half the contents. "Why did you say you'd dropped by?"

"Dropped by?" He shook his head as Laurel leaned back, clutching her cup in both hands. "Laurel, we're supposed to go out to dinner."

"Oh." He was probably right, she thought vaguely. If Jerry said they had a dinner date, they had a dinner date. He kept a very precise appointment book.

"Laurel and I are working on a story," Matt put in more for his own amusement than to rescue Laurel. "We've run into some overtime on it. As a matter of fact, we were, ah, covering ground when you knocked on the door." Not by the slightest flicker did he betray the fact that Laurel's heel was digging into his foot. "Reporting really does interfere with a social life."

"Yes, but—"

"You know what it's like to be on deadline, I'm sure." Matt gave him an easy smile. "Laurel and I probably won't have time for anything more than a cold sandwich. We could be tied up on this for—weeks. You'll give Jerry a call when things calm down, won't you, Laurel?"

"What? Yes, yes, of course." She drained her coffee and wished he'd go so that she could pour another. "I'm awfully sorry, Jerry."

"I understand. Business before pleasure." Matt stopped himself before he choked over his coffee. Jerry rose, setting down his cup before he straightened his tie. "Just ring my office when things are clear, Laurel. And try to cut down on that coffee.''

''Mmm-hmmm,'' was the best she could manage as her teeth were digging into her bottom lip. The door closed quietly behind him. ''Oh God!'' Not sure whether she wanted to laugh or scream, Laurel covered her face with her hands.

''Tacky, Laurellie,'' Matt murmured, pouring out more coffee. ''Leaving it to me to untangle you.''

It would be satisfying to throw the coffee in his face, but she needed it too much. ''With everything that happened today—the story,'' she emphasized firmly when his grin broke out. ''I simply forgot about dinner. And I didn't ask you to untangle me.''

''That's gratitude.'' He tugged on her hair until she looked at him. ''Not only do I let you break three of my toes, but I help you cover up your...impaired condition from your boyfriend.''

''He's not.'' Laurel drank cup number two without a pause, then set down the cup with a snap.

''You're stringing him along.''

''That's not true.'' She started to rise, found it took too much effort and stayed where she was. ''We have a perfect understanding. We're friends. Damn it, he's a very nice man really, just a little...''

''Don't say harmless again, the poor guy doesn't deserve it. Then again, he doesn't seem to be in danger of having his heart broken.''

''Jerry doesn't see me that way,'' Laurel began.

Looking at her, sulky-mouthed and sleepy-eyed, Matt leaned closer. ''In that case, you can leave the pompous off of my earlier description of him.''

Laurel put her hand firmly on his chest. She wasn't about to risk letting the room spin around her again. "I'm going to bed."

The corner of his mouth tilted. "I love aggressive women."

"Alone," Laurel told him, fighting back a laugh.

"Terrible waste," he murmured, taking the hand she held against him to his lips. Turning it over, he brushed them over her wrist and felt the wild beat below the skin.

"Matthew, don't."

He looked at her. It would be easy, so very easy. He had only to draw her to him and kiss her once; they both knew it. She wanted, he wanted, yet neither of them were quite sure how it had come to this. "Years from now, I'm going to hate myself for handling it this way," he murmured as he rose. "I'd take some aspirin now, Laurellie. You're going to need all the help you can get with that hangover in the morning."

Cursing himself all the way, Matt walked to the door, then shut it firmly behind him.

Chapter Five

"Damn you, Bates."

Laurel stared at the pale, wan reflection in her bathroom mirror while hammers pounded dully in her head. Why did he have to be right?

Grabbing a bottle of aspirin, she slammed the door of the medicine cabinet closed. This was followed by a pitiful moan as she clutched her head. Laurel knew it wasn't going to fall off; she only wished it would.

She deserved it. Laurel downed the two aspirins and shuddered. Anyone who drank four martinis in an afternoon deserved what she got. She might have accepted it with some grace if he just hadn't been right.

It didn't help her mood that she could remember what had happened after the drinking. She'd practically thrown herself at him. God, what a fool! He wasn't going to let her forget it. Oh no, he'd tease and torment her for months. Maybe she deserved that too, but... Oh Lord, did she have to remember how wonderful it had been, how unique? Did she have to stand here knowing she wanted it to happen again?

Well, it wasn't. Dragging both hands through her hair, she willed the pounding in her head to stop. She wasn't going to fall for Matthew Bates and make an idiot out of herself. She might be stuck with him on the story, but personally it was going to be hands off and keep your distance. She'd chalk up her reaction to him to an excess of liquor. Even if it wasn't true.

With a sigh, Laurel turned toward the shower. She'd do the intelligent thing. She'd soak her head. As she reached for the tap, the pounding started again—at the front door and inside her temples. Whoever it was deserved a slow, torturous death, she decided as she trudged out to answer.

"Good morning, Laurellie." Matt leaned against the doorjamb and grinned at her. His gaze slid down her short, flimsy robe. "I like your dress."

He was casually dressed, as always, but fresh and obviously clearheaded. She felt as though she'd walked through a desert, eating a few acres along the way. "I overslept," she muttered, then folded her arms and waited for him to gloat.

"Had any coffee yet?"

She eyed him warily as he closed the door. Maybe he was just waiting for the perfect moment to gloat. "No."

"I'll fix it," he said easily and strolled into the kitchen.

Laurel stared after him. No smart remark, no smirk? How the hell was she supposed to keep up with him? she demanded as she dragged herself back to the shower.

She'd been ready to battle, Matt thought as he reached for the glass container of coffee. And all she really wanted to do was crawl back into bed and shut down. A hell of a woman, he thought again. A great deal like her grandmother.

His thoughts traveled back to the evening before. Because he'd known better than to stay in his apartment, one thin wall away from Laurel, Matt had gotten in his car. A little legwork to take his mind off the woman. Olivia Armand would be a fount of information, and her opinion of the Trulanes was bound to be less biased than Laurel's.

Olivia greeted him on her terrace with a look that held both speculation and pleasure. "Well, well, now the evening has possibilities."

"Miss Olivia." Matt took the gnarled, ringed hand in his and kissed it. It smelled of fresh jasmine. "I'm mad about you."

"They all were," she said with a lusty laugh. "Sit down and have a drink, Matthew. Have you softened that granddaughter of mine up yet?"

Matt thought of the fiery woman he'd held only an hour before. "A bit," he murmured.

"You're slow, boy."

"I've always thought a man's more successful if he covers all the angles first." He handed her a drink before he sat down beside her.

"Not joining me?"

"It's hard enough to keep a clear head around you." While she laughed, he sat back and lit a cigarette. "Where's Susan?"

"Upstairs, being shocked by my journals."

"What'd you think of her?"

Olivia took a slow sip. Little fingers of moonlight danced over the diamonds on her hands. Insects buzzed around the hanging lantern by the door, tapping against the glass. The scents from the garden beyond rose up lazily. "Bright girl. Well bred, a bit shaky and sad, but strong enough."

"She claims her sister was murdered."

The thin white brows rose, more Matt observed, in thoughtfulness than surprise. "So that's what this is all about. Interesting." She took another sip, then tapped her finger against the glass. "The poor girl was bitten by a snake in the swamps behind Heritage Oak. Tell me why Susan's thinking murder."

In the brisk, concise style he used in his reporting, Matt ran through the entire events of the day. He saw a bat swoop low over the trees, then disappear. The air was full of the sounds of crickets and the occasional croak of a frog. Palm fronds rustled overhead. The breeze carried a teasing scent of magnolia. A long way from New York, he mused.

"Not as cut and dried as the Trulanes like to keep things," Olivia commented. "Well, Matthew, murder and mystery keep the blood moving, but you're not telling me this to keep my arteries from hardening."

He grinned. She could always make him grin. Leaning back, he listened to the sounds of the night. "I know the general background on the Trulanes, and Laurel gave me a few more details—through rose-colored glasses," he added.

"A touch of jealousy's a healthy thing," Olivia decided. "Might get you on your horse."

"The point is," Matthew said dryly, "I'd like you to tell me about them."

"All right. We'll walk in the garden. I get stiff sitting so long."

Matt took the hand she held out and helped her up. She was tiny, it always surprised him. She walked lightly. If there was any pain or discomfort in her joints, she gave no sign of it. He hadn't lied when he'd said he was mad about her. Within five minutes of their first meeting, he'd fallen for her, and had had no trouble understanding why she'd been the most sought-after girl, then woman, then widow, of the parish.

"Marion was finished in France," Olivia began. "There were rumors of an ill-fated love affair, but she'd never talk about it. She's quiet, but she's sharp, always was. For all her good works and elegant airs, she's also a snob. I'm fond enough of the girl, but she's not her mother as some would like to think."

Matt laughed, patting the hand tucked through his arm. "I knew I could count on you for a straight shot, Miss Olivia."

"Can't stand pussyfooting around. Now Charles was like his mother," she continued. "Good-looking boy, head in the clouds. But he had talent. He was shy about it, but he had talent. One of his watercolors hangs in my sitting room."

Then he was good, Matt mused. Olivia might buy the attempt of a poor neighbor, but she wouldn't hang it in Promesse d'Amour unless it deserved it.

"I was disappointed in him for running off with his brother's wife." Catching the ironic look in Matt's eye, she wagged a finger at him. "I have my standards, Yankee. If Louis's wife and brother wanted each other, they should have been honest about it instead of sneaking off like thieves in the night. Louis would have dealt with it better."

"Tell me about him."

"Laurel's first love." She cackled at Matt's expression. "Simmer down, Matthew, every woman's entitled to one fairy tale. When he was young, he was a vibrant, exciting man. He was devoted to his family, and his family's business, but he wasn't serious or stuffy. I'd never have abided that. I believed he loved his first wife deeply and the betrayal destroyed him. It didn't help when the rumors started that she'd been carrying Charles's baby."

"Did you ever meet Anne Trulane?"

"No, Louis was selfish with her, and I felt he was entitled." She sighed and broke a blossom from an azalea. "They were planning a party in September. Marion told me it was going to be a huge, splashy affair, introducing

Anne to New Orleans society. She said the poor child was torn between excitement and terror at the idea. I admit, I was looking forward to getting a close look at her. They said she resembled Elise."

"They?" Matt prompted.

"The servants. Bless them." She turned back toward the house, fleetingly remembering a time when she could have walked and run in the garden for hours. "If I want to know what's going on at Heritage Oak, I ask my cook. She'll tell me what their cook told her." She gave a gusty sigh. "I love espionage."

"You remember what Elise Trulane looked like?"

"My memory's twice as old as you are." She laughed, relishing rather than regretting the years. "More."

Despite the lines time had etched, her face was beautiful in the moonlight. The hand under his was dry with age. And strong. "Miss Olivia, where can I find another like you?"

"You've got one under your nose, you slow-witted Yankee." She settled back in her chair with a little sound of pleasure. "Ah, Susan, come out." She gestured to the woman hesitating at the garden doors. "Poor child," she said to Matt, "she's still blushing. How did you like my journals?"

"They're very—colorful. You've had a..." How did one put it? "A full life, Mrs. Armand."

Olivia gave a hoot of laughter. "Don't water it down, child. I've sinned and loved every minute of it."

"A drink, Susan?" Matt steered her to a chair.

"No, thanks. Laurel's not with you?"

"I don't like to bring her when I'm courting Olivia," he said easily, pleased to see that she could smile. "Since I'm here, I wonder if you can remember any names Anne might have mentioned in her letters, anything unusual or out of place she might have written about."

Susan lifted her hands, then let them fall. "She wrote mostly of Louis and the house . . . and Marion, of course. She'd grown fond of Marion. The servants . . . a Binney, a Cajun woman Anne said ran the place." Susan thought back, trying to find the details he wanted. "I got the impression she hadn't really taken over as mistress yet. Anne was a bit overwhelmed by having servants."

"Anyone outside the family?"

"She didn't really know anyone else. Oh, there was one of Louis's accountants, Nathan Brewster. She mentioned him a couple of times. I think he'd come to the house to go over papers with Louis. He made Anne nervous." Susan smiled again, this time with sadness. "Anne was very shy of men. Other than that it was all Louis. He was teaching her to ride. . . ."

"Nathan Brewster," Olivia murmured. "I've heard of him. Sharp boy. Your age, Matthew. Supposed to have a nasty temper, nearly killed a man a couple years back. Seems the man was too friendly with Brewster's sister."

"Anything you don't know, Miss Olivia?"

"Not a damn thing." She grinned and gestured for a fresh drink.

He turned to pour it for her. "Susan, do you have a picture of Anne?"

"Yes, do you want it?"

"I'd like to see it."

When she'd risen to go inside, Matt handed Olivia her drink. "Know anything about the Heritage Oak swamp being haunted?"

"Don't be smug, Matthew," she advised. "We Creoles understand the supernatural more than you Yankees. Most of the swamps are haunted," she said with perfect calm as she swirled her bourbon. "The ghosts in Heritage Oak's date back to before the war."

Matthew settled back down, knowing there was only one war Olivia would feel worth mentioning. He remembered Laurel had done precisely the same thing. "Tell me."

"One of the Trulane women used to meet her lover there. Damned uncomfortable place for adultery," she added practically. When Matthew only laughed, she went on blandly. "When her husband found them, he shot them both—the gun's under glass in their library—and dumped the bodies in quicksand. Since then, occasional lights've been seen or someone'll hear a woman sobbing. Very romantic."

"And terrifying to someone like Anne Trulane," he added thoughtfully.

"It's only a wallet-size," Susan said as she came back out. "But it was taken less than a year ago."

"Thanks." Matt studied the picture. Young, sweet, shy. Those were the words that came to his mind. And alive. He could remember how she'd looked the morning they'd found her. Swearing under his breath, he handed the picture to Olivia.

"I'll be damned," she muttered, tapping the photo against her palm. "She could be Elise Trulane's twin."

The sound of Laurel rummaging in the bedroom brought him back to the present. Matt shifted his thoughts. There was another interview that day. Louis Trulane. He took the coffee out on the gallery and waited for Laurel.

She liked pink begonias, he mused. Pinching off one of the blossoms that trailed over the railing, Matt let the fragrance envelop him. Pink begonias, he thought again. Lace curtains. Where did a man who'd grown up with holes in his shoes fit into that? Strange, he thought more about his beginnings since he'd gotten involved with Laurel than he had in years.

He was staring down into the courtyard when she came out, but Laurel didn't think he was seeing the ferns and flowers. She'd only seen that expression on his face a few times when she'd happen to glance up and see him at his typewriter, immersed in a story. Intense, brooding.

"Matthew?" It was an encompassing question. She wanted to ask what troubled him, what he was thinking of, or remembering. But the look stayed in his eyes when he turned to her, and she couldn't. Then it cleared, as though it had never been.

"Coffee's hot," he said simply.

She went to it, dressed in a sheer cotton skirt and blouse that made him hope the heat wave continued. "No I-told-you-so?" she asked before she sat on one of the white wrought-iron chairs.

"People in glass houses," he returned, leaning back against the railing. "I've had my share of mornings after. Feeling better?"

"Some. I'm going to call the house before we leave. I want to make sure Susan's settling in all right."

"She's fine." Matt speculated on what a woman like Laurel would wear under a summer dress. Silk—very thin silk perhaps. "I saw her and your grandmother last night."

The cup paused on its way to Laurel's lips. "You went out there last night?"

"I can't keep away from your grandmother."

"Damn it, Matthew, this is my story."

"Our story," he reminded her mildly.

"Either way, you had no business going out there without me."

Walking over, he helped himself to a cup of coffee. "As I recall, you weren't in the mood to socialize last night. If you had been," he added smoothly, "we wouldn't have found ourselves at your grandmother's."

Her eyes narrowed at that, and she rose. "Just because my mind was fuzzy yesterday, Bates, don't get the idea in your head that you attract me in the least." Because he only smiled, she plunged on. "*Any* man might look good after four martinis. Even you."

He set down his cup very carefully. "Mind clear this morning, Laurellie?"

"Perfectly, and—" She broke off when he pulled her against him.

"Yes, I'd say your mind was clear." He lowered his mouth to her jawline and nibbled. "You're a woman who knows exactly what she wants, and what she doesn't."

Of course she was, Laurel thought as she melted against him. "I don't want—oh." Her breath shuddered out as he nuzzled her ear.

"What?" Matt moistened the lobe with his tongue, then nipped it. "What don't you want?"

"You to—to confuse me."

She felt the brush of his lashes against her cheek as he made a teasing journey toward her mouth. "Do I?"

"Yes." His lips hovered just above hers. Laurel knew exactly what would happen if they met. She took a step back and waited for her system to level. "You're doing this to take my mind off the story."

"We both know"—he caught her hair in his hand—"this has nothing to do with any story."

"Well the story's what we have to concentrate on." She spoke quickly, had to speak quickly until she was certain the ground was steady again. "I don't want you digging without me. I found Susan in the first place, and—"

"Damn it, if and when there's a story you'll get your half of the by-line."

It was easier to be angry than aroused so she let her temper rise with his. "It has nothing to do with the by-line. I don't like you probing Grandma and Susan for leads without me. If you'd told me what you wanted to do, I'd have had some more coffee, a cold shower and pulled myself together."

"Maybe you could have." Sticking his hands in his pockets, he rocked back gently on his heels. "The point is I wanted to talk to someone about the Trulanes, someone who has a little objectivity."

She flared at that, then subsided, hating him for being right. "Let's just go," she muttered, whirling away.

"Laurel." Matt took her arm, stopping her at the doorway. "It's not a matter of the story," he said quietly. "I don't want you to be hurt."

She stared at him while her guards began to shift on their foundations. Trouble, she thought. I'm really going to be in trouble. "I asked you before not to be nice to me," she murmured.

"I'll give you a hard time later to make up for it. The way you feel about Louis—"

"Has nothing to do with any of this," she insisted, no longer certain either of them were speaking of the story. "Let me deal with it myself, Matthew. I can."

He wanted to press her, for himself, for what he needed from her. The time would come when he would have to. "Okay," he said simply. "Let's go."

The breeze helped. It whispered soothingly through the windows as they drove out of town. With her head back and her eyes shut, Laurel listened to Matt's accounting of his visit to her grandmother the evening before.

"I take it from that scornful tone in your Yankee voice that you don't believe in the Trulane ghosts?"

"And you do?" Grinning, he sent her a sidelong look. When she didn't answer right away, he slowed down to look at her more carefully. "Laurel?"

She shrugged, then made a business out of smoothing her skirts. "Let's just say I've got Creole blood, Matthew."

He couldn't stop the smile, on his lips or in his voice. "Ghosts, Laurel?"

"Atmosphere," she corrected, goaded into admitting something she'd just as soon have kept to herself. "I've been in that swamp. There're flowers where you least expect them, small patches of prairie, blue herons, quiet water." She turned in her seat so that the breeze caught the tips of her hair and carried them out the window. "There's also quicksand, nasty little insects and snakes. Shadows." Frustrated, she turned to stare through the windshield. "I never liked it there. It's brooding. There're places the sun never reaches."

"Laurel." Matt stopped the car at the entrance to Heritage Oak. "You're going by childhood impressions again. It's a place, that's all."

"I can only tell you how I feel." She turned her head to meet his eyes. "And apparently how Anne Trulane felt."

"All right." Shifting into first he maneuvered the car between the high brick pillars. "But for now, let's concentrate on human beings."

The oaks lining the drive were tall and old, the Spanish moss draping them gray green and tenacious. It hadn't changed. And, Laurel realized at the first sighting, neither had the house.

The brick had aged before she'd been born. There were subtle marks of time, but they'd been there as long as she could remember. The lines of the house were sharp and clean, not fluid like Promesse d'Amour, but no less beautiful. The brick was a dusky rose, the balconies soft black. Their delicacy didn't detract from the arrogance of the house. If Laurel saw her own ancestral home as a woman, she saw Heritage Oak as a man, bold and ageless.

"It's been a long time," she murmured. Emotions raced through her—memories. Knights and tea parties, filmy dresses and pink cakes. She'd been a child the last time she'd seen it, daydreamed in it.

With a sigh, Laurel turned and found her eyes locked with Matt's. There were new emotions now, not so soft, not so tender. This was reality, with all its pain and pleasure. This was real. Too real. Giving into the panic of the moment, Laurel fumbled with the door handle and got out of the car.

What was happening to her? she asked herself as she took three long, deep breaths. It was getting to the point where she couldn't even look at him without wanting to run—or to reach out. A physical attraction was no problem. She'd managed to submerge that feeling for a year. This was something else again and it promised not to be so easily dealt with. She was going to have to, Laurel told herself, just as she was going to have to deal with her feelings for the Trulanes.

"Matthew, let me handle this." Calmer, she walked with him to the wide, white porch. "I know Louis and Marion."

"Knew," he corrected. He hadn't missed the way she'd looked at the house. Or the way she'd looked at him. "People have the inconsiderate habit of changing. I won't make you any promises, Laurel, but I won't interfere until I have to."

"You're a hard man, Bates."

"Yeah." He lifted the knocker and let it fall against a door of Honduras mahogany.

A tall, angular woman answered the door. After a brief glance at Matt, her nut-colored eyes fastened on Laurel. "Little Miss Laurel," she murmured and held out both thin hands.

"Binney. It's so good to see you again."

Josephine Binneford, housekeeper, had weathered the decade since Laurel had last seen her with little change. Her hair was grayer but still worn in the same no-nonsense knot at the back of her neck. Perhaps there were more lines in her face, but Laurel didn't see them.

"Little Miss Laurel," Binney repeated. "Such a fine, beautiful lady now. No more scraped knees?"

"Not lately." With a grin, Laurel leaned over to brush her cheek. She smelled of starch and lilac. "You look the same, Binney."

"You're still too young to know how fast time goes." Stepping back, she gestured them inside before she closed out the brilliant sunshine and heat. "I'll tell Miss Marion you're here." With a gait stiffened by arthritis, she led them to the parlor. *"Revenez bientôt,"* she murmured, turning to Laurel again. *"Cette maison a besoin de jeunesse."* Turning, she headed up the stairs.

"What did she say?" Matt asked as Laurel stared after her.

"Just to come back again." She cradled her elbows in her hands as if suddenly cold. "She says the house needs youth." She crossed into the parlor.

If people change, she thought, this remains constant. The room could have been transported back a century; it would look the same in the century to come.

The sun gleamed through high windows framed with royal blue portieres. It shone on mahogany tables, drawing out the rich red tints. It sparkled on a cut-glass vase that a long-dead Trulane bride had received on her wed-

ding day. It lay like a lover on a porcelain woman who'd
been captured for eternity in the swirl of a partnerless
waltz.

Matt watched Laurel's long, silent survey of the room.
The play of emotions on her face had him dealing with
frustration, jealousy, need. How could he get her to turn
to him when so much of her life was bound up in what had
been, who had been.

"Memories are nice little possessions, Laurel," he said
coolly. "As long as you don't ignore the present when you
take them out to play."

He'd wanted to make her angry because her anger was
the easier thing for him to deal with. Instead, she turned
to him, her eyes soft, her face stunning. "Do you have any,
Matthew?" she asked quietly. "Any of those nice little
possessions?"

He thought of a roof that leaked and icy floors and a
plate that never had enough on it. He remembered a
woman hacking, always hacking, in her bed at night,
weakening already weak lungs. And he remembered the
promise he'd made to get out, and to take the woman with
him. He'd only been able to keep the first part of the
promise.

"I have them," he said grimly. "I prefer today."

She'd heard something there, under the bitterness. Vulnerability. Automatically, Laurel reached out to him.
"Matthew..."

Not that way, he told himself. He'd be damned if he'd
get to her through sympathy. He took the hand she held
out, but brought it to his lips. "Life's a ridiculous cycle to
be involved in, Laurellie. I've always thought making
memories has more going for it than reliving them."

She dropped her hand back to her side. "You're not
going to let me in, are you?"

"Today." He ran his fingers through her hair. "Let's concentrate on today."

Unaccountably hurt, she turned from him. "There isn't any without a yesterday."

"Damn it, Laurel—"

"Laurel, I'm sorry to keep you waiting." Marion glided in as only a woman taught to walk can do. She wore filmy dresses in pastels that always seemed to float around her. As Laurel took her hands, soft and small, she wondered how anyone could be so coolly beautiful. Marion was nearing forty, but her complexion was flawless with a bone structure that spoke of breeding. Her scent was soft, like her hands, like her hair, like her eyes.

"Marion, you look lovely."

"Sweet." Marion squeezed her hands before releasing them. "I haven't seen you since that charity function two months ago. It was odd seeing you there with your pad and pencil. Are you happy with your career?"

"Yes, it's what I've always wanted. This is a colleague of mine, Matthew Bates."

"Nice to meet you, Mr. Bates." Marion held his hand an extra moment, hesitating while her eyes searched his face. "Have we met?"

"Not formally, Miss Trulane. I was here when your sister-in-law was found last month."

"I see." Briefly, her eyes clouded with pain. "I'm afraid I don't remember too much of that day clearly. Please sit down. Binney is seeing to some refreshments. Louis will be along in a moment." She chose a Hepplewhite for herself, straight-backed and dully gleaming. "He's tied up on the phone. Actually, I'm glad to have a moment with you before he comes." Marion folded her hands on her lap. "Laurel, you haven't seen Louis in a very long time."

"Ten years."

"Yes, ten years." Marion gazed out of the window a moment, then sighed. "One loses track of time here. I had to stop having you over after Charles and Elise...went away. Louis wasn't in a proper state for an impressionable young girl."

Ten years, Laurel thought, and it still hurts her. What has it done to him? "I understand that, Marion. I'm not a girl anymore."

"No, you're not." Her gaze shifted back, away from the trim lawn and oaks. "Laurel, you saw only the beginnings of a change in him, but as the months passed, as the years passed, he became bitter," she said briskly. "Given to flashes of temper, of absentmindedness. There were times he wouldn't remember—" She stopped herself again, unlacing her hands. "He didn't forget," she corrected with a wistful smile. "He simply chose not to remember. He and Charles were—well, that's done."

"Marion, I know how difficult it must've been for him." Laurel reached out to lay a hand on hers. "I always knew. The truth is, I didn't stay away because you didn't ask me to come, but because I knew Louis wouldn't want me here."

"You always understood a great deal," Marion murmured. With a sigh, she tried to shake off the mood. "When he brought Anne home, no one was more surprised, more pleased than I. She'd taken that hard edge away."

"I felt that too." She smiled when Marion sent her a questioning look. "I phoned him a few weeks after he was married."

Nodding, Marion laced her hands again. Her nails were oval, unpainted and buffed. "Perhaps he was overprotective, possessive, but Anne was so young, and he'd been hurt so badly. I'm telling you this now because I want you"—her gaze shifted to Matt—"both of you to understand the state Louis is in now. There's been so much pain in his life. If he seems cold and remote, it's only his way of dealing with grief." She turned her head as Binney wheeled in a tea tray. "Ah, ice tea. Do you still take too many sugars, Laurel?"

She smiled. "Yes. Oh." She glimpsed the tiny pink cakes arranged on the tray. "How sweet of you, Binney."

"I only told the cook Miss Laurel was coming for tea." She gave Laurel a quick wink. "Don't eat more than three or your grandmother will scold me."

Laughing, Laurel bit into one as the housekeeper left the room. The light, sweet taste brought back a new flood of memories. She heard ice tinkle in the glasses as Marion poured. "Binney hasn't changed. The house either," she added with a smile for Marion. "I'm so glad."

"The house never changes," Marion told her as she offered Laurel fresh, cold tea in a Waterford glass. "Only the people in it."

Laurel didn't hear him, but sensed him. Carefully, she set down the glass she held. Turning her head, she looked into Louis's eyes.

Chapter Six

Can ten years be so long? she thought with a jolt. She'd thought she was prepared. She'd hoped she was. There was gray in his hair now, near the temples. That she would have accepted. There were lines in his face going deep around his mouth and eyes. She could have accepted them too. But the eyes had none of the warmth, none of the humor she'd loved so much.

He was thin, too thin. It made him look older than thirty-six. She rose, and with a mixture of pain and pity, went to him. "Louis."

He took her hand and the ghost of a smile touched his mouth. "Grown up, Laurel? Why did I expect to find a child?" Very lightly, he touched a fingertip to the underside of her chin. She wanted to weep for him. "You always promised to be a beauty."

Laurel smiled, willing the warmth to come to his eyes. "I've missed seeing you." But the warmth didn't come, and his hand dropped away. She felt his tension even before she felt her own. "Louis, this is my associate, Matthew Bates."

Louis's eyes flicked over Matt and grew colder. "I believe we've met."

"Some tea, Louis?" Marion reached for the pitcher.

"No." His voice was curt, but Marion made no sign other than a quick compression of lips. Neither man noticed as their eyes were on Laurel. "We're not here for tea and cakes this time, are we, Laurel?" Louis murmured before he crossed the room to stand in front of the empty hearth. Over it was an oil of his mother. Laurel remembered it well. It had been there for years, except for a brief period when Elise Trulane's portrait had replaced it. "Why don't we get on with this?" Louis suggested. "I agreed to see you and Mr. Bates to put an end to this rumor Susan started." He gave Laurel a long look. "Ask your questions. I used to have all the answers for you."

"Louis . . ." She wanted to go to him, soothe him somehow, but the look in Matt's eyes stopped her. "I'm sorry to intrude this way. Very sorry."

"It isn't necessary to be sorry." Louis drew out a thin cigar, eyeing it for a moment before lighting it. "Nothing ever remains as it was. Do what you came to do."

She felt her stomach tighten. The power in him was still there, a power she'd recognized even as a child. It had driven him to take up the reins of a multimillion-dollar firm before he'd finished college. It had enabled him to enchant a young girl so that the woman could never forget him. But it was so cold now. Laurel stood where she was in the center of the parlor while the gap between memory and today grew wider.

"Susan is certain that Anne would never have gone out into the swamp alone," she began, knowing she began badly. "Susan claims that Anne had a terror of dark places, and that the letters she'd written expressed a specific fear of the place."

"And she believes Anne was forced to go in there," Louis finished. "I know all of that already, Laurel."

She was a journalist, she had an assignment. She had to remember it. "Was Anne afraid of the swamp, Louis?"

He drew on his cigar and watched her through the cloud of smoke. "Yes. But she went in," he added, "because she died there."

"Why would she have gone in?"

"Perhaps to please me." Carelessly he flicked cigar ash into the scrubbed hearth. "She'd begun to feel foolish about this fear she'd dragged along since childhood. When I was with her," he murmured, "she wouldn't need a light on in the hallway at night." Abruptly, his head lifted again, to the arrogant angle Laurel remembered in a young man. "The story about the ghosts in the swamp had her imagining all sorts of things. I was impatient." He drew on the cigar again, harder. "She had a...need for my approval."

"You think she might have gotten up in the middle of the night and gone out there to please you?" Laurel asked him, taking a step closer.

"It makes more sense than believing someone broke in, dragged her out and left her without myself or any of the servants hearing a sound." He gave her another cool, uncompromising look. "You read the police report, I imagine."

"Yes." She moistened her lips as she remembered the photograph. "Yes, I did."

"Then there's no need for me to go over that."

"Did your wife often have trouble sleeping?" Matt put in, watching as a very small muscle worked in Louis's jaw.

"Occasionally. Particularly when I was working." He glanced over Matt's head, out the long windows. "She thought she'd seen lights in the swamp."

"Did anyone else see them?"

Louis's mouth twisted into something like a smile. "Over the years, dozens of people have claimed to—usually when they've kept company with a bottle of bourbon.''

"Mr. Bates," Marion broke in. "Anne was afraid of the swamp, but she was also fascinated with it. It's not unusual for someone to be fascinated by something they fear. She'd become obsessed by the legend. The problem...the blame," she amended slowly, "comes from none of us taking her seriously enough. She was so young. Perhaps if we'd insisted she go in during the daylight, she wouldn't have felt compelled to go in at night."

"Do you think she was capable of going in there alone, at night?" Laurel asked her.

"It's the only explanation. Laurel, we all loved her." She sent Louis a quick, misty look. "She was sweet and soft, but she was also highly strung. I thought her nerves came from the plans we were making for the party."

"What difference does it make now?" Louis demanded and tossed his cigar into the hearth. It bounced, then lay, smoldering. "Anne's gone, and neither Susan nor her letters can change it."

"The letters were stolen from Susan's room," Laurel said quietly.

"That's ridiculous. Who would steal letters? She misplaced them." Louis dismissed them with an angry shrug.

"You were married for nearly a year," Matt said casually. "Yet none of your closest neighbors had met your wife. Why?"

"That's my business."

"Louis, please." Laurel took another step toward him. "If we could just understand."

"Understand?" he repeated, and stopped her with a look. "How can you? She was hardly more than a child, the child you were when I last saw you. But she didn't have your confidence, your boldness. I kept her to myself be-

cause I wanted to. I had to. There was a generation between us."

"You didn't trust her," Laurel murmured.

"Trust is for fools."

"Isn't it odd," Matt commented, drawing Louis's fury
from Laurel to himself, "how much Anne resembled your
first wife."

The only sound was Marion's sharp intake of breath.
Though his hands clenched into fists, Louis stood very
still. Without another word, another look, he strode out.

"Please, Louis just isn't himself." Marion fiddled
nervously with the glasses. "He's very sensitive about
comparisons between Anne and Elise."

"People are bound to make them," Matt returned,
"when the physical resemblance is so striking."

"More than physical," Marion murmured, then went on
in a rush. "It was a natural observation, Mr. Bates, but
Louis won't discuss Elise and Charles. If there's nothing
else...?"

"Do you know Nathan Brewster?" Laurel asked
abruptly.

Marion's eyes widened before her lashes swept down.
"Yes, of course, he's one of Louis's accountants."

Matt's brow lifted before he exchanged a look with
Laurel. "His was one of the few names Anne mentioned
in her letters."

"Oh, that's natural, I suppose. He came to the house a
few times on business. It's true Anne didn't meet many
people. Well." She rose, sending them both an apologetic
smile. "I'm sorry I couldn't be of more help, but perhaps
you can put Susan's doubts to rest now." She held out her
hands to Laurel again. "Come back soon, please, just to
talk like we used to."

"I will. Tell Louis..." Laurel sighed as she released Marion's hands. "Tell him I'm sorry."

They walked out of the house in silence, drove away in silence. As the frustration, the anger built, Matt swore to himself he'd say nothing. Whatever Laurel was feeling was her own business. If she let her emotions get in the way, let herself grieve, there was nothing he could do about it.

On an oath, he yanked the wheel, skidded to the side of the road and stopped.

"Damn it, Laurel, stop."

She kept her hands very still in her lap and stared straight ahead. "Stop what?"

"Mourning."

She turned her head then, and though her eyes were dry, they were eloquent. "Oh, Matthew," she whispered, "he looked so lost."

"Laurel—"

"No, you don't have to say it. He's changed. I expected it, but I wasn't ready for it." She drew a deep breath that came out trembling. "I wasn't ready to see him hurting so much."

Cursing Louis Trulane and all he stood for, Matt gathered Laurel close. She didn't protest when he cradled her against him, but held on. The sun streamed into the car. She could hear birds calling and chattering in the trees beyond the car. As he stroked her hair, she closed her eyes, letting herself draw from the comfort he offered.

"I am mourning," she murmured. "I don't know if you can understand just how important Louis was to my childhood, my adolescence. Seeing him like this today..." With a sigh, she kept her head on his shoulder and watched the patterns sun and shade made on the road.

"You're thinking of him as a victim, Laurel. We're all victims of what life deals out. It's how we handle it that's important."

"When you love someone, and you lose them, it kills something in you too."

"No." He let himself breathe in the scent of her hair. "Damages. We all have to deal with being damaged one way or the other."

He was right, of course he was right. But it still hurt. She said nothing, but sat quietly with her cheek on his shoulder while his hand trailed through her hair. His body was so firm, his heartbeat so steady. She could lose herself here, Laurel realized, in the front seat of his car with the sun pouring through and the sound of birds calling lazily from tree to tree.

"I keep telling you not to be nice to me," she murmured.

He tilted his head back to look at her. His eyes were intense again, seeing too much. His fingers spread to cup her face. When her mouth opened, he tightened them. "Shut up," he told her before he pressed his lips to hers.

Not so light this time, not so gentle. She tasted frustration and didn't understand it. But she also tasted desire, simmering, waiting, and couldn't resist it. Her body went fluid, every bone, every muscle as she surrendered to whatever it was they needed from each other. The need was there, she knew. Had always been there. The more she had resisted it, fought it, ignored it, the stronger it had become until it threatened to overpower every other. Food, air, warmth, those were insignificant needs compared to this. If she was seduced, it wasn't by soft words or skilled kisses, but by the emotions that had escaped before she'd been able to confine them.

"Matthew." She dropped her head on his shoulder and tried to steady her breathing. "This isn't—I'm not ready for this."

Smoldering with impatience and desire, he forced her head back. "You will be."

"I don't know." She pressed her hands to his chest, wishing he could understand—wishing she could. "I told you that you confuse me. You do. I've never wanted a man before, and I never expected it to be you."

"It is me." He drew her closer. "You'll just have to get used to it." His expression changed slowly from barely restrained temper to intentness. "Never wanted a man," he repeated. "Any man? You haven't—been with any man?"

Her chin came up. "I said I never wanted one. I don't do anything I don't want to."

Innocent? Dear God, he thought, shouldn't he have seen it? Sensed it? Gradually, he loosened his grip until he'd released her. "Changes the rules, doesn't it?" he said softly. Matt took out a cigarette while she sat frowning at him. "Changes the rules," he repeated in a whisper. "I'm going to be your lover, Laurellie. Take some time to think about it."

"Of all the arrogant—"

"Yeah, we'll get into that in depth later." He blew out a stream of smoke. She was steadier now, he thought ruefully. He was wired. He'd better give them both some time to think about it. "Let me throw a couple of theories at you on Anne Trulane."

He started the car again while Laurel struggled to control her temper and to remember priorities. The story, she told herself, and forced her jaw to unclench. They'd deal with this . . . personal business later. "Go ahead."

He drove smoothly, ignoring the knot of need in his stomach. "Louis married Anne Fisher because she looked like his first wife."

"Oh really, Matthew."

"Let me finish. Whether he cared for her or not isn't the issue. Once they were married he brought her back to Heritage Oak and kept her there, away from outsiders. Men. He didn't trust her."

"He'd been hurt before, in the cruelest possible way."

"Exactly." Matt pitched his cigarette out the window. "He was obsessed with the idea that she might find a younger man. He was possessive, jealous. What if Anne rebelled? What if she gave him a reason to doubt her loyalty?"

"You're suggesting that Louis killed her because he thought she'd violated his trust." She didn't like the chill that brought to her skin, and turned on him. "That's ridiculous. He isn't capable of killing anyone."

"How do you know what he's capable of?" he tossed back. "You didn't know that man in the parlor today."

No, she didn't, and the truth stung. "Your theory's weak," she retorted. "Look at the time table. Anne died between 12:00 and 4:00 A.M. Louis woke the household sometime between two and three."

"He could've taken her in before two," Matt said mildly. "Maybe he never intended for her to die. He might've wanted to frighten her, taken her in and left her there."

"Then why would he call out a search party?"

Matt turned his head, letting his gaze skim over her face before he shifted it back to the road. "He could've forgotten he'd done it."

Laurel opened her mouth and closed it again. Absentminded, Marion had said. He'd been absentminded, angry, bitter. She didn't like the picture it was drawing in her mind.

Laurel remained silent as he drove through downtown traffic. No man forgot he'd left his wife alone and lost. No sane man. Matt swung over to the curb and stopped. "Where are we going?"

"To see Nathan Brewster."

Laurel glanced up at Trulane's, one of the oldest, most prestigious buildings in the city. Perhaps they'd find something in there that would shift the focus from Louis. "Marion didn't want to talk about Nathan Brewster."

"I noticed." Matt stepped out of the car. "Let's find out why."

"I know what you're thinking," she murmured as they walked toward the front doors.

"Mmmm. That could be embarrassing."

She shot him a look as they walked inside. "Anne was attracted to Nathan Brewster, acted on it and Louis found out. Rather than dealing with it or divorcing her, he drags her into the swamp in the middle of the night and dumps her."

Matt checked the board on the wall and located Accounting. "It crossed my mind," he agreed.

"You've got your own prejudices against Louis."

"You're damned right," he muttered and took her hand to pull her to the elevator. "Look," Matt began before she could retort. "Let's talk to the man and see what happens. Maybe he's just been embezzling or having an affair with Marion."

"Your ideas get more and more ludicrous." She stepped into the elevator and crossed her arms.

"You're sulking."

"I am not!" Letting out an exasperated breath, she glared at him. "I don't agree with your theory, that's all."

"Give me yours," Matt suggested.

She watched the numbers flash over the elevator door. "After we talk to Brewster."

They stepped out on carpet, thick and plush. Without giving Matt a glance, Laurel crossed to the receptionist. "Laurel Armand, Matthew Bates, with the *Herald*," she said briskly. "We'd like to see Nathan Brewster."

The receptionist flicked open her book. "Do you have an appointment?"

"No. Tell Mr. Brewster we'd like to speak with him about Anne Trulane."

"If you'll have a seat, I'll see if Mr. Brewster's available."

"Nice touch, Laurellie," Matt told her as they crossed the reception area. "Ever think about the military?"

"It's gotten me into a lot of city officials." She took a seat under a potted palm and crossed her legs.

He grinned down at her. There wasn't a trace of the sad, vulnerable woman who'd rested her head on his shoulder. "You've got style," he decided, then let his gaze sweep down. "And great legs."

Laurel slanted him a look. "Yeah."

"Mr. Brewster will see you now." The receptionist led them down a hallway, past an army of doors. After opening one, she went silently back to her desk.

Laurel's first impression of Nathan Brewster was of sex. He exuded it, ripe, physical. He was dark, and though he wasn't tall, he had a blatant virility no woman could miss. Good looks, though he had them, didn't matter. It was his primitive masculinity that would either draw or repel.

"Ms. Armand, Mr. Bates." He gestured toward two small leather chairs before taking a seat behind his desk. "You wanted to talk to me about Anne Trulane."

"That's right." Laurel settled herself beside Matt as she tried to reason out what kind of reaction a woman like Anne would have had to Nathan Brewster.

"She's dead," Brewster said flatly. "What does the press have to do with it?"

"You met Anne at Heritage Oak," Laurel began. "Not many people did."

"I went there on business." He picked up a pencil and ran it through his fingers.

"Could you give us your impression of her?"

"She was young, shy. My business was with Mr. Trulane; I barely spoke to her."

"Strange." Matt watched Brewster pull the pencil through his fingers again and again. "Yours was one of the few names that came up in Anne's letters." The pencil broke with a quiet snap.

"I don't know what you're talking about."

"Anne wrote to her sister about you." Matt kept his eyes on Brewster's now, waiting, measuring. "Her sister doesn't believe Anne's death was an accident."

Matt watched the little ripple of Brewster's throat as he swallowed. "She died of a snakebite."

"In the swamp," Laurel put in, fascinated by the waves of frustration and passion pouring out of him. "Did you know she was frightened of the swamp, Mr. Brewster?"

He shot Laurel a look, molten, enraged. Matt's muscles tensed. "How would I?" he demanded. "How would I know?"

"Why would you suppose she'd go into a place that terrified her?"

"Maybe she couldn't stand being locked up anymore!" he exploded. "Maybe she had to get out, no matter where, or how."

"Locked up?" Laurel repeated, ignoring the tremor in her stomach. "Are you saying Louis kept her a prisoner?"

"What else can you call it?" he shot back at her. His hands clenched and unclenched on the two jagged pieces of pencil. "Day after day, month after month, never seeing anyone but servants and a man who watched every move she made. She never did anything without asking him first. She never stepped a foot beyond the gates of that place without him."

"Was she unhappy?" Laurel asked. "Did she tell you she was unhappy?"

"She should've been," Nathan tossed back. "Trulane treated her more like a daughter than a wife. She needed someone who'd treat her like a woman."

"You?" Matt said softly. Laurel swallowed.

Brewster's breathing was labored. The temper Matt had been told of was fighting to get free. He'd have to struggle to control it. And, Matt mused, he wouldn't often win.

"I wanted her," Brewster said roughly. "From the first time I saw her out on the lawn, in the sunlight. She belonged in the sunlight. I wanted her, loved her, in a way Trulane couldn't possibly understand."

"Was she in love with you?"

Matt's quiet question drew the blood to Brewster's cheeks. "She would have left him. She wouldn't have stayed in that—monument forever."

"And come to you?" Laurel murmured.

"Sooner or later." The eyes he turned on Laurel were penetrating, filled with passion and feeling. "I told her she didn't have to stay locked up there, I'd help her get away. I told her she'd be better off dead than—"

"Better off dead than living with Louis," Laurel finished as his harsh breathing filled the room.

"It must've been frustrating," Matt continued when Brewster didn't answer. "Loving your employer's wife, rarely being able to see her or tell her how you felt."

"Anne knew how I felt," Brewster bit off. "What difference does it make now? She's dead. That place killed her. He killed her." Brewster sent them both a heated look. "Print that in your paper."

"You believe Louis Trulane killed his wife?" Matt watched Brewster sweep the remains of the pencil from his desk.

"He might as well have held a gun to her head. She got away," he murmured as he stared down at his empty hands. "She finally got away, but she didn't come to me." The hands curled into fists again. "Now leave me alone."

Laurel's muscles didn't relax until they'd walked out into the sunlight. "That was a sad, bitter man," she murmured.

"And one who takes little trouble to hide it."

She shivered, then leaned against the side of his car. "I can understand why he made Anne nervous."

Matt cupped his hands around a match as he lit a cigarette. "Give me a basic feminine reaction."

"Passion, virility, primitive enough to fascinate." She shook her head as she stared up at the ribbons of windows. "For some women, that would be irresistible simply because it's rather frightening. A woman like Anne Trulane would've seen him as one of her dark closets and stayed away." With a short laugh, she dragged a hand through her hair. "I'm not a psychiatrist, Matthew, but I think a certain kind of woman would be drawn to a man like Brewster. I don't believe Anne Trulane would've been."

Letting out a long breath, she turned to him. "It's my turn to write a scenario."

"Let's hear it."

"Brewster's in love with her—or thinks he is, it wouldn't matter with a man like him. He tells Anne, asks her to leave Louis for him. How would she feel? Frightened, appalled. A little flattered perhaps."

He cocked a brow, intrigued. "Flattered?"

"She was a woman," Laurel said flatly. "Young, unsophisticated." She glanced back up at the windows, thinking of Brewster. "Yes, I believe she might have felt all three emotions. It confuses her, he pressures her. He's very intense, dramatic. She loves her husband, but this is something she doesn't know how to cope with. She can't even write her sister about it."

Matt nodded, watching her. "Go on."

"Suppose Brewster contacts her, demands to see her. Maybe he even threatens to confront Louis. She wouldn't have wanted that. Louis's approval and trust are important to her. Anne had to know about his first wife. So..."

Laurel's eyes narrowed as she tried to picture it. "She agrees to see him, meets him outside, late while Louis is working. They argue because she won't leave Louis. He's a physical man." She remembered his strong fingers on the pencil. "He's convinced himself she wants him but is afraid to leave. He drags her away from the house, away from the light. She's terrified now, of him, of the dark. She breaks away and runs, but it's dark and she's in the swamp before she realizes it. She's lost. Brewster either can't find her or doesn't try. And then..."

"Interesting," Matt murmured before he flicked his cigarette away. "And, I suppose, as plausible as anything else. I wish we had those damn letters," he said suddenly. "There must be something there or they wouldn't've been taken."

"Whatever it was, we won't find it there now."

Matt nodded, staring past her. "I want to get into that swamp, look around."

Laurel felt the shudder and repressed it. "Tonight?"

"Mmmm."

She supposed she'd known it was bound to come down to this. Resigned, she blew the hair out of her eyes. "Let's go get some mosquito repellent."

He grinned and ran a finger down her nose. "Only one of us has to go. You stay home and keep a light burning in the window."

The brow went up, arrogant, haughty. "My story, Bates. I'm going; you can tag along if you want."

"Our story," he corrected. "God knows if there'll be anything in there but a bunch of filthy insects and soggy ground."

And snakes, Laurel thought. She swallowed, tasting copper. "We'll have to see, won't we? Matthew, we're running out of angles."

They stared at each other, frowning. Dead end—for now.

"Let's get some lunch," Laurel suggested as she swung around to get into the car. "And get back to the paper before we're both out of a job."

Chapter Seven

Laurel spent over an hour with Matt in the newspaper morgue, going through files and crosschecking until her neck ached. With luck, the *Herald* would be on computers within the year. Laurel might miss the ambience of the cavernous morgue with the smell of dust and old paper, but she wouldn't miss the inconvenience. Some of the staff might grumble about having to learn the tricks of a terminal, the codes, the ways and means of putting in and taking out information at the punch of a button. She promised herself, as she rubbed at a crick in the back of her neck, she wouldn't be one of them.

"Brewster made page two with his fists," Laurel murmured as she scanned the story. "Two years ago last April." She glanced up briefly. "No one's memory's quite like Grandma's."

"She mentioned a sister."

"That's right. His sister'd been seeing a man who apparently liked his bourbon a bit too well. He'd seen her in a bar with another man and made a scene—tried to drag her out. Brewster was there. It took roughly ten men to pull him off, and before they did, he'd broken a couple of tables, a mirror, three of the guy's ribs, his nose and jaw and his own hand."

Matt lifted a brow at her cool recital of the violence. "Charged?"

"Assault headed the list," Laurel told him. "Ended up paying a fine when his—ah—opponent wouldn't press charges." She scrawled a note on her pad. "Apparently once Brewster's temper is lost, it's lost. I think I'll see if I can trace the sister. He might have talked to her about Anne."

"Mmm-hmm."

She glanced over to see Matt scribbling quickly in his own book. "What've you got?"

"Speculation," he murmured, then rose. "I have a few calls to make myself."

"Matthew," Laurel began as they started down the corridor, "weren't you the one who had all the big talk about sharing?"

He smiled at her, then pushed the button for the elevator. "After I make the calls."

"Make up your own rules as you go along?" she muttered when they stepped inside the car.

He looked down at her, remembering her passion in his arms, the vulnerability in her eyes. Her innocence. "I might just have to."

Laurel felt the quick chill race up her spine and stared straight ahead. "Let's stick with the story, Bates."

"Absolutely." Grinning, he took her arm as the elevator opened. They walked into the city room and separated.

Reporters have to get used to rude replies, no replies, runarounds. Laurel dealt with all three as she dialed number after number in an attempt to trace Kate Brewster. When she finally reached her, Laurel had to deal with all three again.

Brewster's sister flatly refused to discuss the barroom brawl and had little to say about her brother. At the mention of Anne Trulane, Laurel sensed a hesitation and caught a slight inflection—fear?—in Kate's voice as she claimed she didn't know anyone by that name.

Laurel found herself dealing with another hazard reporters face. An abrupt dial tone in the ear. Glancing up, she saw Matt cradling his own phone between his shoulder and ear as he made notes. At least one of us is getting somewhere, she thought in disgust as she rose to perch on the corner of his desk. Though she tried, it wasn't possible to read his peculiar type of shorthand upside down. Idly, she picked up the styrofoam cup that held his cooling coffee and sipped. When she heard him mention the name Elise Trulane, she frowned.

What the hell's he up to? Laurel wondered as he easily ignored her and continued to take notes. Checking up on Elise...he's hung up on the similarity in looks, she decided. What does a runaway first wife have to do with a dead second one? As an uncomfortable thought raced into her mind, Laurel's eyes darted to Matt's. *Revenge?* But that would be madness. Louis wasn't—Louis couldn't... From the way he returned the look, she realized Matt read her thoughts while she wasn't able to penetrate his. Deliberately, she turned away to stare into Don Ballinger's office. The information they'd given their editor may have been sketchy, but it had been enough to give them the go-ahead.

Matt hung up and tapped his pencil on the edge of his desk. "What you get?"

"Zero, unless you count the impression that Anne Trulane's name made Brewster's sister very nervous. And another impression that she treads very carefully where her brother's concerned. What're you up to, Matthew?"

He ran the pencil through his hands, but the gesture had none of the nervous passion and energy that Brewster's had. His hands were lean, not elegant like Louis's, she thought, or violent like Brewster's. They were capable and clever and strong—just as he was. Disturbed, she shifted her gaze to his face. It was becoming a habit for thoughts of him to get in the way of what they had to do.

"Matthew?" she repeated as he looked beyond her.

"It seems the two Mrs. Trulanes had one or two things more in common than looks," he began. He dropped the pencil on his desk and drew out a cigarette. "They each had only one relative. In Elise's case, it's an aunt. I just spoke with her."

"Why?"

"Curiosity." He blew out a stream of smoke as a reporter behind them swore and hung up his own phone. "She describes her niece as a shy, quiet girl. Apparently Elise loved Heritage Oak, and unlike Anne, had already begun to take over the position of lady of the manor. She enjoyed the planning, the entertaining, had ideas for redecorating. The aunt was astonished when Elise ran off with Louis's brother—hasn't seen or heard from her since. She thought Elise was devoted to her husband."

"So did everyone else," Laurel commented. "Things like that do happen, Matthew, without anyone on the outside being aware. I don't imagine Elise would've told her aunt or anyone else that she was having an affair with Charles."

"Maybe not. There is something I find interesting," he murmured, keeping his eyes on Laurel's. "Elise inherited fifty thousand dollars on her twenty-first birthday. She turned twenty-one the month after she left Heritage Oak. The money," he said slowly, "was never claimed."

Laurel stared at him while ideas, answers spun through her mind. "Maybe she—she might've been afraid to claim it thinking Louis could trace her."

"Fifty thousand buys a lot of courage."

"I don't see what digging into Elise's business has to do with Anne."

His eyes were very calm, very direct. "Yes, you do." She looked pale again, drained as she had that morning. Smothering an oath, Matt rose. "It's something to think about," he said briskly. "For now, we'd better concentrate on what we have to do tonight. Let's go home. We can catch a couple of hours' rest before we have to get ready."

"All right." She didn't want to argue, and though it was cowardly, she didn't want to think about what he'd just told her. There'd been enough that day. If she were to win out over her emotions, she needed the time to do it.

Matt didn't press her, but made easy, innocuous conversation on the drive home. He was good at falling back on a relaxed style to conceal his inner thoughts and feelings. It was one of his greatest professional weapons, and personal defenses. If he was furious with Laurel's automatic and unflagging defense of Louis Trulane, it wasn't apparent. If he harbored frustrating, near-violent urges to take her to some dark, private place until she forgot Louis Trulane existed, he didn't show it. His voice was calm, his driving smooth. His muscles were tight.

"A nap," Laurel said as they left his car to cross the courtyard, "sounds like heaven. It's been a long two days."

A long year, he thought as needs crawled in him. "And it's going to be a long night," he said easily.

She smiled at him for the first time since they'd left the *Herald*. "What time do we go on safari?"

"Midnight's the accepted hour, I believe." He touched the tips of her hair, then started up the steps.

"Garlic doesn't work against ghosts, does it?" Laurel mused. "No silver bullets, wooden stakes. What does?"

"Common sense."

She gave a windy sigh. "No romance."

At the top of the steps, he grinned at her. "Wanna bet?"

Laughing, she bent to pick up a wrapped box at the base of her door. "I don't remember ordering anything."

"From Jerry no doubt—a box of number-two pencils."

She tried to glare at him and failed. "Midnight, Bates." After a brief search, she found her keys and unlocked the door. With a final arch look, she closed the door in his face.

His grin faded as he started down to his own apartment. The woman was driving him crazy. She had to be blind not to see it, he thought as he jabbed his key into the lock. Maybe he'd been too cautious. As he walked into the kitchen, Matt stripped his shirt over his head and tossed it aside. Then again, it had taken him weeks to get used to the fact that he'd been struck by lightning the first time she'd lifted those dark green eyes and looked at him.

At that point, he'd told himself it was impossible, the same way it had been impossible for him to lose his head over the neatly framed photograph Curt had put on their shared desk in their college dorm.

"My sister," Curt had said in his abstracted way. "Runs copy at my father's paper during the summer. Guess you'd know about things like that."

The words hadn't registered because Matt had to concentrate on just breathing. There he'd been—a senior in college, a man who'd already seen and worked his way through more than many men do in a lifetime—rooted to the spot with one of the shirts he'd been unpacking dangling from his hand, head swimming over a girl who couldn't have been more than fifteen. Impossible.

Matt grabbed some orange juice from the refrigerator and chugged straight from the bottle. He'd gotten over that first . . . whatever it had been quickly enough. Or he'd told himself he had. But when William Armand had written him, all those years later, mentioning his relationship to Matt's senior-year college roommate and offering a position on the *Herald,* Matt hadn't hesitated. And he hadn't asked himself why.

It would've helped, he thought as he tossed the empty bottle in the trash, if he'd found a slow brain underneath that fabulous face. Or a bland or too sweet personality. It would've helped if he hadn't sat next to her for a full year knowing she was everything he'd ever wanted.

He intended to have her, though her innocence urged him toward a traditional courtship—quiet dinners, candlelight, a gentle touch. Matt felt the stir of desire, and swore. He hoped he had the control he was going to need.

He intended to have her, though the difference in their backgrounds sometimes reared up to mock him. He'd already pushed his way through a lot of doors; now he had to make sure his luck held.

He was going to have her.

Matt stuck his hands in his pockets and headed for the shower. And he heard her scream.

Later, he wouldn't remember bursting out of his own apartment and rushing to hers. He'd remember hearing her scream again, and again, but he wouldn't remember beating on her door and finally in desperation knocking it in. What he would remember, always, was the way she'd looked, standing frozen with her hands at her own throat, her face like parchment and her eyes terrified.

"Laurel!" He grabbed her, spinning her around and into him where she stood in his arms, rigid as a stone. "What? What is it?"

He could feel the beat of her heart. Was it possible for a heart to beat that fast? Her skin was like ice, dampened by a sheen of sweat, but she didn't tremble. Not yet. "The box," she whispered. "In the box."

With one hand still on her arm, he turned and looked into the box on the table. The oath ripped out under his breath, pungent. "It's all right, Laurel. It's dead, it can't hurt you." His body trembled with fury as he lifted a portion of the copperhead from the box. "It can't hurt you now," he repeated, turning back to see her staring, transfixed at what he held in his hand. Sweat pearled on her forehead. Through her parted lips, her breath came harsh and quick.

"Matthew... please."

Without a word, he covered the box and carried it from the apartment. He returned—twenty, thirty seconds later— to find her leaning, palms down on the table, head lowered, weeping. He still didn't speak as he picked her up to carry her to the sofa and cradle her like a baby. Then the trembling started.

Five minutes... ten, and he said nothing, only holding her as she wept into his bare shoulder and shuddered. She seemed so small. Even when he'd seen those flashes of vulnerability he would never have imagined her like this— totally helpless, without the slimmest defense against anything or anyone. As he held her close, Matt promised himself when he found out who'd sent the box, he'd make them pay for it.

Safe. She knew she was safe now, though the fear kept threatening to bubble up again—that awful, strangling fear that couldn't be described but felt only. She could feel his heartbeat under her hand, and the warm flesh. He was holding her, and the world would settle again.

"I'm sorry," she managed, but continued to cling to him.

"No, don't." He kissed her hair, then stroked it.

"It's always been like that. I was bitten once. I can't remember it, or being sick, but I can't, I just can't handle—"

"It's all right. It's gone now, don't think about it anymore." The trembling had nearly stopped, but he could feel the occasional spasm that passed through her. Her breath still came in hitches. His skin was damp from her tears. He wanted to make her forget—he wanted to get his hands on whoever had done this to her. "Let me get you a brandy."

"No." She said it too quickly, and the hands against his chest balled into fists. "Just hold me," she murmured, hating the weakness, needing his strength.

"As long as you want." He heard her sigh, felt her fingers relax. The minutes passed again, long and silent so that he thought she slept. Her breathing had evened, her heartbeat slowed and she was warm again. He knew if she'd needed it, he could have held her just so for days.

"Matthew..." His name came on a sigh as she tilted her head back to look at his face. Her eyes were still puffy, her skin pale. He had to fight the wave of emotion to keep his fingers from tightening on her. "Don't go."

"No." He smiled and traced a finger down her cheek. Her skin was still damp, still warm from her weeping. "I won't go."

Laurel caught his hand in hers and pressed it to her lips. Matt felt something wash over him, warm and sweet, that he didn't yet recognize as tenderness. She saw it move in his eyes.

This was what she'd been waiting for, Laurel realized. This was what she'd needed, wanted, refused to consider. If he would ask her now—but he wouldn't, she knew it. The asking would have to come from her.

"Make love with me," she whispered.

"Laurel..." Her words stirred him, impossibly. How could he take her now when she was utterly without defense? Another time, oh God, another time, he'd have given anything to hear her say those words. "You should rest," he said inadequately.

He's not sure of himself, she realized. Strange, she'd thought he was always so sure. Perhaps his feelings for her were as confusing as hers for him. "Matthew, I know what I'm asking." Her voice wasn't strong, but it was clear. "I want you. I've wanted you for a long time." She slipped her hand up over his chest and neck to touch his cheek. "Love me—now." She brought her lips to his as if quietly coming home.

Perhaps he could have resisted his own need. Perhaps. But he couldn't resist hers. He drew her closer with a moan, gathering her against him as his mouth told her everything in silence. She was boneless, so pliant it seemed she might simply melt out of his arms like a mirage he'd traveled to over endless, impossible days and nights only to find it vanished. He deepened the kiss with something like panic, but she remained, warm and real against him.

Her mouth tasted of woman, not of visions, so warm and sweet he had to fight the urge to devour it. Her tastes, that small hand that remained on his cheek, the airy scent, merged together to make his senses swim. He couldn't afford the luxury now, not this first time.

Matt buried his face at her throat, struggling to hold on to some slim thread of control, but his lips wouldn't be still. He had to taste her. His hands roamed up and over subtle curves. He had to touch her.

"Laurel..." He slipped her loosened blouse off one shoulder so that his lips could wander there. "I want you— I ache with it."

Even as he told himself to move slowly, he was drawing the blouse from her. She shifted to help him, murmuring, then only sighed.

"Not here." He closed his eyes as her lips brushed his throat. "Not here," he said again and rose with her still in his arms. This time she'd let herself be led. She rested her head on his shoulder as he carried her into the bedroom.

The lights slanted through wooden shutters. It highlighted his eyes, so suddenly intense, as he laid her on the bed. "I won't hurt you."

She smiled and reached for him. "I know."

The mattress sighed as he lay beside her. With her eyes just open, she could see the play of light while his lips traced over her face. It was so easy. She should have known that with him it would be so easy. Running her palms, then her fingertips over his back, she felt the ripple of muscle, the taut skin, the strength. This had attracted her from the beginning, and she had struggled to ignore it. Now, she could take her fill.

He caressed her with his lips. Caressed. She hadn't known such a thing was possible with lips alone. He showed her. Her skin softened, then tingled from it.

Lazily... thoroughly...

His mouth moved over her throat and shoulders while his hands tarried nowhere but in her hair. A gentle nip, a soft flick of tongue and she was floating.

She heard the bluesy sound of a trumpet from outside. The sound drifted into the room to mix in her mind with Matt's murmurs. He nuzzled into her throat so that she turned her head to give him more freedom and breathed in the sweet scent of vanilla from her bedside candle. She made some sound, a long low sigh, but had no way of knowing that this alone had his pulses hammering.

His lips pressed onto hers with the edge of desperation under the gentleness. She felt it, yielded to it, as she drew him yet closer.

When he touched her, a lean, hard hand over the silk of her camisole, her sigh became a moan. She arched, feeling the aching fullness in her breasts she'd never experienced. Needs sprang up from everywhere, all at once, to pulse under her skin. But he wouldn't be rushed—by her or himself. His fingers trailed, aroused, but stopped just short of demand. He wanted the demand to come from her own needs, not his.

Slowly, inch by inch, he drew the swatch of silk down to her waist, finding her skin no less luxurious. With open-mouthed kisses he explored it, listening to the shuddering sound of her breathing that meant the loss of control. He wanted that from her, for her, while he desperately hung on to his own. When his mouth closed over her breast, the muscles in his back relaxed. God, she was sweet.

While Laurel went wild beneath him, he lingered, drawing out their mutual pleasure, drinking in her tastes and textures. He caught her nipple between his teeth, holding it prisoner, tormenting it with the play of his tongue until he knew she was utterly steeped in passion, in the dark, mindless pleasures. Then he went on.

She knew only sensations now—there were no thoughts, no sane thoughts as flames leaped inside her and fire shivered along her skin. The movements of her body were instinctive, offering, pleading. His lips continued to roam over her as he slipped the rest of her clothes from her. The feel of hot flesh against hot flesh had her gasping. With each trembling breath she took, the scent they made together overwhelmed her. Intimate, earthy. Glorious.

Her body was molten—fluid, fiery—but she was helpless. Whatever he wanted from her he could have taken in whatever way he chose. The choices she had made—first to resist him, then to accept him—no longer applied. There were no choices in this world of dazzling light and radiant heat. Her body craved. Her spirit hungered. She was his.

He knew it. And, knowing, fought to remember her innocence when her passion was tearing at his control. She was agile and slim, and at the moment as abandoned as a sleek young animal. Her hands sought him without hesitation, her lips raced to take whatever he'd allow. With his breath rasping, his blood pounding, he struggled to keep the pace as he'd begun. Easy.

When he touched her, she jolted beneath him, shuddering and shuddering with the first peak. Through his own desire, Matt could feel her stunned, helpless delight. No one else had given her this, no one else had taken this from her. No one.

He buried his face at her throat, groaning. So moist, so warm. So ready. He shifted onto her. "Laurel..."

Suspended on shaft after shaft of sensation, she opened her eyes and looked into his. If her body was fluid, his was tight as a bowstring. Over the waves of passion came one clear certainty. He thought only of her. She couldn't speak, drowned by needs and the sharply sweet newness of love just discovered. Laurel drew his mouth down to hers.

At the touch of her lips, she gave up her innocence as easily, as gently, as sliding down a long cool bank toward a warm river.

She slept. Matt lay beside her and watched the light through the window slats go from white, to rose, to gray before the moonlight drifted thinly in. His body was exhausted, from the strain of control, from the ultimate loss of it, but his mind wouldn't rest.

There'd been times over the last months when he'd nearly convinced himself that once he'd had her, the lingering need would pass. Now, as he lay in her bed, with moonlight slanting across her body, with her head nestled against his shoulder, he knew the need would remain as basic and essential as the need for air.

Physically he knew she was his. He could touch off her passion, exploit her needs and keep her. It wasn't enough. He wondered if he could draw out her emotions, her love, with the same deliberate care with which he'd drawn out her desire. He wondered if he had the patience he'd need.

Turning his head, he looked down at her as she slept against him. Her skin was like porcelain with the dusky lashes shadowing her cheeks. Delicate... He traced a finger down her cheekbone. Yes, she had delicacy which at times made him feel like an awkward boy staring at pastries in a bakery window. But she had verve, and energy and ambition. These he understood, as they matched his own.

Partners, he thought, and his eyes glinted with something between amusement and determination. Damn right they were. Bending down, he crushed his mouth to hers.

Head swimming, body throbbing, Laurel came awake on a wave of passion. Her skin leaped under his hands as they raced over her, taking and demanding with a speed that left her giddy. She moaned against his mouth, tossed so quickly from gentle sleep to ruthless desire that she could only cling. He set the pace again, but it was nothing like the first time. She catapulted from peak to peak, swept along, driven, until he took her with all the urgency he'd blocked out before.

Spent, stunned, she waited for her breath to return as he lay over her, his face buried in her hair. Should she have known it would be like this? Could she? More than anything, that quick, desperate loving showed her just how careful he'd been with her the first time.

I love him, she thought as she tightened her arms around him. Wouldn't that knock him off his feet? With a wry smile, she toyed with the hair that curled over his neck. Matthew Bates, I'm going to play a very careful hand with you—and I'm going to win.

She gave a long, luxurious sigh. Did loving make the body feel so wonderfully lazy? "Were you trying to tell me it's time to get up?" she murmured.

Lifting his head, he grinned at her. "I don't think so."

"This wasn't supposed to happen."

"Yes, it was." He kissed her brow lightly, lingeringly. "We're just a little ahead of schedule."

Her brow arched, but the haughty gesture had to compete with the soft, just-loved flush of her skin. "Whose schedule?"

"Ours," he said easily. "Ours, Laurel."

It was difficult to argue with something that seemed so reasonable. Laurel linked her hands at the base of his neck and tilted her head. "You look good, Bates."

Amusement flickered in his eyes. "Yeah?"

"Yeah." She ran her tongue over her teeth. "I guess I'm getting used to those beachboy looks and that Yankee speech pattern. Or maybe"—she caught her bottom lip between her teeth but the laughter shone in her eyes—"maybe I just like your body. You work out?"

He braced himself comfortably on his elbows. "Now and again."

Experimentally, Laurel pinched his bicep. "Weights?"

"No."

"Well, I've never cared for obvious muscles." She ran a hand down to his wrist, then back again. "You seem to be in good enough shape to handle our plans for the evening."

He nipped at her bottom lip. "Which are?"

"A little hike through the swamp."

He rubbed his lips over hers easily while his mind did some quick calculations. He could distract her, wait until she slept again, then go without her. "I was thinking we could...postpone that."

"Were you?" Though her body began to soften, her mind was much too sharp. "Until you could sneak out there on your own?"

He should've known better. "Laurel..." He slid a hand up to her breast.

"Oh no." She shifted quickly until she lay on top of him. "You can forget the idea of going out there without me, Bates. We're a team."

"Listen." He took her firmly by the shoulders while her hair dipped down to brush his. "There isn't any need for you to go. It's just a matter of poking around anyway. It'll be faster and easier with only one of us."

"Then you stay here." She kissed him briskly and sat up.

"Damn it, Laurel. Think."

"About what?" she tossed back as she rose, naked, to rummage through her drawers.

"No one left a nasty little box at my door."

She bit down hard on her lip, then turned with a T-shirt and a pair of panties in her hand. "No, they didn't," she said calmly enough. "They left it at mine, obviously for a reason. We're making someone nervous, Matthew. And that someone is damn well going to have to deal with me."

He looked at her, small and straight with her naked skin glowing in the moonlight. At the moment, she looked perfectly capable of avenging herself. "Okay, tough guy," he drawled as he swung his legs out of bed. "When we find out who it was, you can go a few rounds. In the meantime, you might remember there're snakes in that swamp—and they're not dead in a box.''

He knew he'd been deliberately cruel, he'd meant to be. But when he saw her fingers tighten on the shirt she held, he cursed himself.

"I won't look." Jaw set, she wriggled into the panties. "You'd better get dressed."

"Stubborn, hardheaded, obstinate," he began furiously.

"Yeah." Jerking the shirt over her head, Laurel glared at him. "But not stupid. Whoever dropped that thing at my door wanted me to back off. That points to Brewster or—or the Trulanes," she managed after a moment. "If they wanted us to back off, there's a reason, and the reason might just be in that swamp."

"You won't get any argument on that from me," he said evenly. "But it doesn't follow that you have to go."

"If I let that kind of threat steer me away, I'll have to turn in my press badge. Nobody's going to put me in that position." She gave him a long, level look. "Nobody."

Matt's temper struggled toward the surface, then subsided. She was right—that was one point he couldn't get around. In silence, he pulled on his jeans. "I've got to get a shirt, and a flashlight," he said briefly. "Be ready in ten minutes."

"All right." She made a business of searching through her drawers until she was sure he'd gone.

Laurel pressed her fingers to her eyes and let the fear out. It was a sticky, cloying sensation that rolled over her and left her lightheaded. As it ebbed, she rested her hands against the dresser and just concentrated on breathing. She had to go—now more than before she'd looked in that box. If a threat wasn't answered, then it was buckled in to. If there was a threat, it meant someone was afraid.

Anne Trulane had been afraid of the swamp. Laurel pulled on worn jeans with hands that were almost steady again. She understood that kind of fear, the kind that has no true explanation but simply is. Laurel didn't believe Anne had voluntarily walked into that dark, secret place any more than she herself would voluntarily walk into a snake exhibit. The full certainty of it hadn't struck until tonight, with the burgeoning of her own fear. And, by God, she was going to prove it.

Matt . . . Laurel switched on the bedroom light and began to search through the disorder of her closet for boots. He was only being unreasonable because he was concerned for her. While she could appreciate it, she couldn't allow it. Love might urge her to give in to him on this one thing—but then how many other things might she give in to once she started?

However he felt about her, she mused as she located one boot, he felt about her because of the way she was. The best thing she could do for both of them was to stay that way.

Swearing at her own disorganization, Laurel shouldered her way into the closet for the other boot.

When he returned, Matt found her sitting on the floor of her room, fighting with knotted laces. He was wearing an outfit very similar to hers, and his more customary amiable expression. He'd calmed down considerably by rationalizing that she'd be safer with him in any case—and by promising himself he'd watch Laurel like a hawk every moment they were in the swamps of Heritage Oak.

"Having a problem?"

"I don't know how this happened," she muttered, tugging on the laces. "It's like somebody crawled in there, tied these in knots, then buried the boot under a pile of junk."

He glanced at her littered floor. "I'm disillusioned. I always thought you were very precise and organized."

"I am—at work. Damn!" She scowled at a broken nail, then fought with the laces again. "There—now I just need a flashlight." Springing lightly to her feet, she dashed past him and into the kitchen.

"You know, Laurellie," Matt commented as he followed her. "A few more molecules missing and you wouldn't have a seat in those pants."

"It'll be dark."

He patted her bottom. "Not that dark."

Grinning, she pulled a flashlight from the kitchen drawer and tested it. "Then you'll have to walk in front and keep your mind off my anatomy."

"I'd rather watch your back pockets jiggle." Swinging an arm around her, he walked to the door.

"They don't jiggle." She stopped, frowning at the splintered wood. "How did that—"

"You were too busy screaming to open the door," Matt said easily, nudging her outside. "I called the super about it."

"You broke it down?" Laurel turned to stare at him.

He grinned at her expression before he tugged her down the stairs. "Don't make doors like they used to."

He broke it down. The thought of it stunned her, sweetly. At the foot of the stairs she stopped and wrapped her arms around his waist. "You know, Matthew, I've always had a soft spot for knights on white chargers."

He framed her face with his hands before he kissed her. "Even tarnished ones?"

"Especially."

Chapter Eight

Matt parked his car in the shadow of the wall that encircled the Trulane estate. The moment he cut the engine, silence fell. He could sense, though she climbed from the car as he did, Laurel's regret over the one thing they'd carefully not talked about. Trespassing, in secret, on what belonged to Louis. He also knew it was something that would continue to remain unsaid. He slipped his flashlight, base first, into his back pocket.

"I'll give you a leg up first."

Nodding, Laurel placed a foot in his cupped hands and reached for the top of the wall. She shinnied up nimbly, then, bracing herself on her stomach, reached a hand down for his. The grip was firm and dry, holding briefly until they lowered themselves on the other side.

"Somehow, I think you've done this sort of thing before," she murmured, dusting her hands on the back of her jeans.

He grinned. "Let's just say I've had to scale a few walls in my career."

"And not all metaphorical," she concluded.

"You'll force me to mention that you went up and over like a veteran yourself."

Laurel took one brief look around, letting her gaze linger on the shadow of the house in the distance. "I don't suppose you've considered the legal repercussions if we're caught."

It was as close as she'd come, he knew, to speaking of Louis. Matt took her hand, drawing her away from the wall. "Let's not get caught," he said simply.

They moved, as quietly as shadows themselves, over the north lawn. Flashlights weren't needed here. The light of the half-moon was thin, but clear enough to guide the way. The air was still, but far from silent. Night birds rustled in the trees, their whisperings punctuated now and again by the hoot of an owl. Overlaying all was the incessant music of crickets.

Fireflies glimmered with their sporadic gold-toned light. It smelled thickly of summer blossoms and green grass.

Already Laurel could see the gloomy silhouette of the edge of the swamp. The aversion was so ingrained she had to force herself not to hesitate. But her fingers curled tightly around Matt's. His palm was cool and dry against hers.

Doesn't he feel it? she wondered as the chill raced over her skin. Doesn't he feel the *darkness* of the place? It held secrets best left alone—secrets that bred in the soggy grasses. She shuddered as the lawn gave way to it.

"It's a place," Matt said quietly. "It's just a place, Laurel."

"It's evil," she said so simply he felt a tremor of unease. Then she stepped under the first overhang of trees.

Determination made her force back the fear. Though her fingers remained in his, their grip lightened. "Hard to believe," she began in an easier voice, "even driven by love—or lust—that one of the Trulane woman would have picked this place to cheat on her husband. I think her name was Druscilla."

Matt gave a choked laugh as he pulled out his light. "Maybe Druscilla had a thing for humidity and mosquitos. Now..." He didn't switch the light on, but looked behind him where the outline of the house could just be glimpsed through the trees. "I'd say this is about the most direct spot where someone would enter the swamp if they were coming from the house."

Laurel followed his gaze. "Agreed."

"Then it follows that Anne would most likely have come in somewhere around this point."

"It follows."

"Okay, let's go see what we can find. Stick close."

"An unnecessary warning, Matthew," Laurel said loftily as she unpocketed her flashlight. "If you feel something crawling up your back, it's just me."

They hadn't gone more than three yards when the thick, fat leaves dimmed the moonlight. The shadow of the house was lost behind the tangled hedge of other shadows. Already the wild cane sprang up to block what was within, and what was outside, the swamp. The twin beams of their flashlights cut a path through the dark.

It was a world of clinging dampness, of shadows and whispering sounds that made the flesh creep. Even the smell was damp, with the ripe odor of rotting vegetation. Matt began to understand why Anne Trulane may have been terrorized in there. He wouldn't care to lose his way, alone, in the dark. But he wondered why she'd only gone deeper rather than turning back. Blind panic? He scowled at the crude, overgrown path. Maybe.

She should've gotten the hell out.

"Doesn't make sense," he muttered.

Laurel shone her light off the path where something rustled. Her fingers closed over Matt's wrist and let the light, steady pulsebeat soothe her. "What doesn't?"

"Why didn't she get out?"

Carefully, Laurel turned her light back to the path. It was probably only a possum, not every sound meant snakes. She remembered, uncomfortably, that black bear had often been seen in the northern, forested part of the swamp. "Whatever theory we go by, Matthew, Anne was frightened in here. She panicked, lost her sense of perspective."

"Are you frightened?" He glanced down to where her fingers dug into his wrist.

"No." Sending him a rueful smile, Laurel loosened her hold. "No, I'm way past fear, closing in on terror."

"Could you get out of here?"

"Well I—" She broke off, seizing his hand again. There was a time and place for dignity—and this wasn't it. "You're not leaving me in here, Bates."

"What would you do if I did?"

"I'd murder you the minute I got out."

Grinning, he took her arm as they began to walk again. "How?"

"Poison, I imagine, it's the slowest, most painful way."

"No, how would you get out?"

"I'd—" She swallowed on the notion of having to find her way out alone, then turned around. Shadows, rustling, and the cloying smell of wet earth and rotted grass were all around. There was quicksand, she knew, to the east and to the southwest. "I'd head that way in a dead run," she said, pointing, "hang a right at that stump and keep on going."

"And you'd be out in five minutes," he murmured. He turned his face back to hers. The moonlight caught in his eyes, glinting. "Why did she keep going deeper?"

If she tried to think like Anne, Laurel realized, she'd end up losing what courage she had and bolting. Dragging a hand through her hair, she tried to think coolly instead. "She'd been bitten—maybe she was sick, delirious."

"How fast does the poison work, I wonder." He shrugged, making a note to check on it if it became necessary. "It seems she'd've had time to get out, or at least get closer to the edge."

"They found her by the river didn't they?"

"Yeah." He looked down at her again. "Dead center. When we were searching the place, we'd come across her tracks now and again where the ground was wet enough to hold them. There didn't seem to be any pattern."

Blind panic, he thought again. Yet she hadn't been as frozen as Laurel had been that afternoon. She'd been running, in what had appeared to be a random flight, deeper into what she feared most…or running away from something she found more terrifying.

Laurel jolted as the bushes beside them rustled. Matt aimed his light and sent a raccoon scurrying back into the shadows.

"I hate making an ass of myself," she mumbled as her heart slipped back out of her throat. "Let's go on." Annoyed at the blow to her pride, she started ahead of him.

They moved in silence, going deeper. Laurel kept her flashlight trained on the uneven ground to guide their way while Matt shone his from side to side, searching for something neither of them could name. But they'd both followed hunches before.

"Don't laugh," Laurel ordered, coming to an abrupt halt.

"Okay," he said amiably.

She hesitated, gnawing at her lip. "I mean it, Bates, don't laugh."

"Cross my heart?" he ventured.

"I feel like—something's watching."

"Another raccoon?"

"Matthew—"

"Relax." He cupped the base of her neck in his hand and rubbed, deliberately treating it lightly because he'd felt that trickle between his shoulder blades as well. Ghost stories, he told himself. He was letting Laurel's feelings about the place get to him.

If he'd believed such things he'd have said there was something evil in the twisting shadows, something that would shrink from the sunlight. But he didn't believe in such things. Evil, when it came, came from the human element.

"Too many people have died here," she said, and shuddered.

He touched her neck again, and his hand, his voice were gentle. "Do you want to go back?"

Oh God, yes, she thought, but squared her shoulders. "No, let's go on. You can smell the river now."

As they came near the banks, she could smell the wet leaves, vegetation, but the river made no sound as it flowed slowly. Cypress trees made lumpy shadows. A few slivers of moonlight worked through the overhanging trees and fell palely on the water, but only made it seem darker. A frog plopped into the river as they approached.

There were alligators in there, Laurel thought, wrinkling her nose. Big ones.

"It was here." Matt shone his light on the ground. "Laurel, could you still get out of this place if you had to?"

As she followed the play of his light she was remembering the picture from the police file. Clamping down on her lip, she forced the image from her mind. "Yes, the way we came's the easiest, I imagine, but almost any direction from here would get you out eventually."

"Yeah." He moved around, playing his light on the ground. "Strange that she picked the core of the swamp to give up." He swore in frustration. Nothing here, he thought, nothing here. What the hell had he expected to find? "I'd like to get my hands on those letters."

"Whoever took them would've destroyed them by now if there was anything in them to work with."

"I wonder if Susan—" He broke off as the beam of his light picked up a glimmer. Bending, Matt worked a small piece of metal from the ground.

"What is it?"

"Looks like a broken piece of jewelry. Seen better days." Rising, he turned it over in his hands. "Anne's?"

Laurel took it from him, wiping away some of the caked-on dirt. "I don't know, a month in this place . . ." She shone her light on it as some nagging memory teased the back of her mind. "It looks like the front of a locket—expensive, look how intricate the carving is." The memory lunged toward the front of her mind, then retreated. Laurel shook her head in exasperation. "It's familiar," she murmured. "Maybe it was Aunt Ellen's—Louis could've given it to Anne after they were married."

"We might be able to check it out for what it's worth." Taking it from her, he slipped it into his pocket. Frustrated, he shone his light to the right and down the bank of the river. "Stay here a minute, I want to get a closer look down there."

"For what?"

"If I knew I wouldn't feel like I was chasing wild geese."

"I'll go with you."

"Laurel, it's a bog down there. You've been lucky avoiding snakes this far. Don't press your luck."

She remembered the water moccasins that swam in the river. With a gesture of indifference, she shrugged. "You've got two minutes, Bates. Any longer and I'm coming after you."

"Two minutes." He kissed her lightly. "Stay here."

"I'm not moving."

She watched the beam of his light as he walked away, then made his slippery way down the bank. He didn't know what he was looking for, but she understood his need to do something. All they'd found so far were more questions, and a broken piece of jewelry.

She frowned again, thinking of it. A childhood memory? she wondered, pushing the hair away from her face. Had she seen that locket when it had been bright and clean—against a white dress? Laurel pressed her fingers to her temple as she tried to bring the image into focus. One of Aunt Ellen's lacy party dresses? Frustrated, she dropped her hand.

Another minute, Bates, she told him silently. Why was it the small night noises seemed to grow louder now that he wasn't standing beside her? She shifted uncomfortably as a bead of sweat trickled down her back, leaving a chill in its wake.

It's just this place, she told herself, refusing the urge to look over her shoulder. In an hour we'll be back home and I'll be able to laugh at how I stood here shivering in the heat and imagining goblins at my back. In an hour...

The soft rustle at her back had her stiffening. Damn raccoons, Laurel thought on a wave of self-disgust. She opened her mouth to call for Matt when an arm locked around her throat.

Shock registered first, seconds before her body reacted to it, or the abrupt lack of air. In an instinctive move of self-preservation, Laurel jabbed back with her elbow, only to meet empty space as she was shoved away. Her flashlight spun out of her hand as her body whooshed through wild cane. She landed hard, her head slamming back into the base of a cypress.

At the edge of the river, Matt saw the arch of light, then darkness where he'd left Laurel. He plunged up the bank, cursing the slick grass and shouting her name. When he saw her sprawled, his heart stopped—with the vivid picture of Anne Trulane leaping in his mind's eye. He grabbed her, not gently, and hauled her against him. At her moan, he began to breathe again.

"What the hell're you doing!" he demanded, rolling with the fury fear had given him.

"I'm having a concussion," she managed and shook her head to clear it—a mistake as the ground tilted under her. "Someone pushed me—came up from behind." She reached gingerly to test the bump at the back of her head, then gripped Matt's shirtfront with sudden strength as he started to rise. "Oh no, you're not leaving me here again."

Simmering with rage, straining at impotence, he settled beside her again. "All right, just sit a minute." He ran his fingers through her hair to lift her face to his. "Are you hurt?"

She saw the anger, the concern, the frustration in his eyes. "Not really." She smiled—her head was throbbing, but that was all. "Just a bump. It didn't knock me out; I just saw stars—not unlike the ones I saw the first time you kissed me."

That helped, she thought, feeling the grip of his fingers on her arm relax slightly. But that brooding look was still in his eyes as he searched her face.

"I shouldn't have left you alone."

"Matthew, if you're going to start being macho and guilty, I'll get cranky." Leaning forward, she kissed him. "Let's see if I can stand up."

With his hands cupping her armpits, he pulled her gently to her feet. No dizziness, she thought, waiting a moment. The throbbing was subsiding to an ache.

"It's okay, really," she said when he continued to study her face. "I've had worse bumps."

You won't have any more while I'm around, he swore to himself viciously, but smiled. "I won't make any remarks about hard heads. Now, what did you see—besides stars?"

"Nothing." She let out a frustrated breath. "I was so busy telling myself I wasn't going to be a fool that I wouldn't look around when I heard something rustling in the bushes. The next thing I knew someone had an arm around my throat. I hadn't even started defensive move 21-A when they pushed me into that tree. By the time the stars stopped exploding, you were here and they were gone."

Whatever grim thoughts of revenge worked in his mind, his touch was gentle as he felt the back of her head. "You'll have a bump," he said easily as he forced his jaw to unclench, "but the skin's not broken."

"There's good news."

Tilting her head back to his, he gave her one long, hard kiss. His hands were steady again, but his temper wasn't. "Sure you can walk?"

"If you mean as in out of here, absolutely. I lost my flashlight."

"Buy a new one," he advised as he picked up his own. "It went in the river."

"Oh, that's just great. I only bought it a month ago." She scowled over this as they started back the way they'd come. "Well I guess we found something after all," she murmured.

"Yeah. Someone who knows what we're up to doesn't like it one damn bit. Lovelorn ghosts don't shove people into trees, do they, Laurel?"

"No." And she was thinking, as he was, that the house was close. The people in it knew the swamp.

They walked back in silence, each of them more cautious than before, listening to every sound, second-guessing the shadows. Matt kept Laurel at his side, his hand on hers until they walked into the clear. There wasn't the faintest glimmer of light from the house in the distance.

The lingering distaste for where they'd been clung to him even after they'd dropped on the other side of the wall. He wanted a shower—a long one.

Laurel didn't speak again until Heritage Oak was miles behind them.

"We'll have to talk to Louis and Marion again."

"I know." Matt punched in the car lighter. Maybe if he filled his lungs with smoke he'd stop tasting the air of the swamp. "Tomorrow."

Leaning back, Laurel closed her eyes. And tomorrow was soon enough to think about it. "I don't know about you, but I'm starving."

He turned his head to look at her. She was still a bit pale—but even that could've been the moonlight. Her voice was steady, her breathing calm. He hadn't sensed fear in her, not even when she'd been half-dazed and sprawled on the ground. Frustration, yes, annoyance with herself for being caught unaware. But no fear.

With her head back and the shadows dancing over her face, she reminded him forcibly of Olivia. Unique, indomitable, fascinating. Laughing, Matt grabbed her hand and pressed it to his lips.

"We'll order a pizza and take it back home."

Though she hadn't a clue what had lightened his mood so abruptly, Laurel went with it. "With everything," she demanded.

It was after two when Laurel pushed away from Matt's smoked-glass table, stuffed. She couldn't say his apartment wasn't what she'd expected because she'd had no idea just what to expect. She did know it showed an easy mode of living—deep, plump cushions, thick carpet, soothing colors all mixed together with a flair for style and a penchant for comfort.

There were neither framed newsprints on his walls nor Picassos but a set of oils done by an artist she didn't recognize. Both were of New York, one a cityscape showing its elegance and glitz, the other a street scene with crumbling buildings and cracked sidewalks. Both were excellent in their way, and the contrasts intrigued her. She supposed, in his career there, he'd have seen both sides.

"I've reached my limit," she said when Matt started to slide another piece onto her plate.

"Big talk about eating it, box and all." Matt bit into the slice he'd offered her.

Picking up her wineglass, Laurel rose to wander the room. Her feet sank into the carpet. "I like your place. You like"—she wiggled her bare toes—"to be comfortable."

"Most people do." He watched as she wandered to his stereo to sort through his album collection.

"Mmmm. But not everyone makes an art out of it." Laurel set a record aside to study the paintings more closely. "These are very good," she commented. "I don't recognize the artist, but I have a feeling I'll be seeing his work again."

"He'd be glad to hear it." Matt picked up his own glass, studying her over the rim. The wine was heavy and sweet. "We grew up in the same neighborhood."

"Really?" Laurel tilted her head, even more interested. "Do you miss it? New York?"

Matt's gaze flicked up to the painting, then back to the wine in his glass. "No."

"But you carry it with you."

"We all carry our baggage around," he murmured, then got up to stick what remained of the pizza in the refrigerator.

Laurel frowned after him. What brought that on? she wondered, then looked back at the paintings. The same neighborhood, she mused, seeing the soiled streets and tired buildings. When he came out of the kitchen she was still facing them. "You grew up here."

He didn't have to see which painting she was looking at to know what she meant. "Yeah." He pulled his shirt over his head as he walked. "I need a shower."

"Matthew." Laurel went after him, catching his arm outside the bathroom door. She recognized impatience and ignored it. "It was hard, wasn't it?"

"I survived," he said indifferently. "Not everyone does."

Her sympathy was automatic and reflected in her eyes, the touch of her hand on his arm, her voice. "Tell me about it."

"Just leave it."

She stared at him, the hurt unexpected and brutally sharp. Her step back was a retreat from it before she straightened her shoulders. "All right, I'm sorry. Thanks for the pizza, Bates. I'll see you in the morning."

He took her arm to stop her. "Laurel, you know you can't stay in your place until the door's fixed."

She met his eyes calmly. "Not all of us needs locks and bolts, Matthew."

"Damn it—" He broke off, making a savage effort to keep his temper. He knew he was wound up, still tense from what had happened to her in the swamp, still dazed by what had happened between them in her bed. Emotions were crowding him, and he wasn't dealing with them well. "Listen, I grew up in a tough little neighborhood on the East Side. It has nothing to do with you. Nothing."

A dash of salt for the wound, Laurel thought as she stared up at him. "That's clear enough," she said evenly. "Let's just call it professional curiosity and leave it at that."

"Damn it, Laurel." He grabbed her by the shoulders when she started to leave again. "You're not staying in that place alone tonight."

"Don't you tell me what I'm going to do."

"I *am* telling you," he tossed back. "And for once you're going to *do* what you're told."

She gave him a cold, neutral look. "Take your hands off me."

He started to get angry, but even through his own anger he could see beneath hers to the hurt. On a sigh, he dropped his forehead to hers. "I'm sorry."

"You don't owe me an apology," she said carefully.

"I do." When he lifted his head, his eyes were dark and thoughtful. "I hurt you, I didn't mean to."

"No, it's all right." Without fuel her temper vanished, leaving only a faint echo of the hurt. "I was prying."

"No, I—" Matt hesitated, then let it go. He wasn't ready to drag it all out and look at it again, not with Laurel. "I don't want to argue with you, Laurel. Look, it's late, we've both had enough to deal with today. I can't dig back there tonight."

Her arms went around him. Even if the anger had still lashed at her, she couldn't have stopped them. "No more questions tonight."

"Laurel…" He covered her offered mouth with his. The tension began to drain, degree by degree, as he filled himself with her. "Stay here," he murmured. "Stay with me."

With a sigh, content, accepting, she rested her head on his shoulder. "Do I get shower privileges?"

She heard his low laugh as he nuzzled at her throat. "Sure. But we have to double up. You've heard about the water shortage."

"No, not a word."

"Really?" He tugged her into the bathroom. "It's at a crisis stage. Let me tell you about it."

She was laughing as he drew her shirt over her head.

When she got out of the shower, Laurel was flushed and tingling. Clutching a towel at her breasts, she looked up at Matt. "I'm so impressed." When his grin tilted, she went on blandly, "With the fact that you're such a conservationist."

"Conservation is my life." He tugged the towel from her, smiling easily when she gasped. "Gotta cut back on the laundry too. You know how many gallons of water a washing machine uses?" His eyes swept down her, then up again. "Better get you into bed, you'll catch a chill."

Regally, she walked away, leaving Matt to admire the view. "I suppose turning on a light would go against your values."

"Civic duty," he corrected, then surprised her by grabbing her around the waist and tumbling onto the bed with her.

Winded, she glared up at him. "Now listen, Bates—"

He silenced her quickly, completely and effectively. He'd meant to tease her, continue the half-torturous, half-pleasurable game they'd begun under the cool spray of the shower. But her legs were tangled with his, her body yielding, and her mouth...

"Oh God, Laurel, I need you." His mouth crushed back on hers with a savagery the night seemed to have worked on him.

He forgot patience, and she, the need for it. He forgot gentleness, and she, the need for it. His tongue dived deep into her mouth as if there were some taste, some hint of flavor he might be denied. But she would have denied him nothing. Her passion raced from tingling arousal to raging desire, and her mouth was as greedy, as insistent as his. She was not to be seduced this time, or to be swept helplessly along, but to take as much as she gave.

She hadn't known passion could strip every remnant of civilization away, but she learned. Glorying in the abandon, she touched and tasted where she would with hands and lips that moved quickly, with no more patience than his. He smelled of the soap she'd lathered on him herself. The sharp, clean scent played with her senses, swam in her head while her needs delved in darker places.

They were only shadows in the bed, tangling, clinging, but their passion had substance and form. Perhaps the whispering threats of the past hours drove them both to take, and take hungrily all that could be found between man and woman. Damp skin, thundering pulses, breathless moans. For both of them it was the moment, the heady present that mattered. Yesterday and tomorrow were forgotten.

He knew he was rough, but control had vanished. Heat seemed to pour out of her, drawing him deeper and deeper into his own furious passion. Her body was as it had been when he'd first taken her hours—oh God, had it only been hours?—before. Sleek and smooth and agile. But the change came from within. There was no pliancy in her now but an urgency and demand that raced with his.

His lips rushed over her, running low on her stomach with hungry kisses. But his need to taste wasn't any stronger than her need to experience. She wanted all there was to have this time, everything he'd already given her and whatever secrets were left. She wanted to learn whatever desire had left to teach.

She opened for both of them, eager, urging him down until he found her. She arched, stunned and only more desperate at the play of his tongue. He whipped her up and over the first crest, never pausing, relentless, as she shuddered with her nails digging into his shoulders.

Wave after wave of heavy, molten pleasure swept her but he continued as if he would keep her, keep them both spinning on the very verge of fulfillment. There couldn't be so much. But even as the thought raced through her mind there was more. And still more. She should have been sated from it, but she pulsed with energy. She should have been overwhelmed, but it was as if, somehow, she'd always known it would be like this. His heart raced with hers, beat matching beat. Passion poured out of her, but as it poured it was replenished.

"Matthew." His name was a moan, a gasp. "I want you."

As his mouth hurried back, skimming over her, she felt his tremors and the hammer-thrust beat of his heart. Each rasping breath seemed to merge with her. She saw his eyes glimmer once in the pale light of the moon, then tasted the mixture of soap and salt on his flesh.

"I need you...." They spoke together. She arched to meet him.

Chapter Nine

The sky hung low. Thick, pewter clouds trapped the heat and humidity so that rain wouldn't have been a threat, but a blessed relief. The leaves didn't stir, or turn their pale undersides up in anticipation, but hung limply.

Laurel leaned back and let the sticky air coming through the car window do what it could. Along the sides of the road the trees stood, casting shade that could offer only slight relief to the throbbing heat. Glancing at them she wished she were sitting under one, near a cool river on soft, damp grass.

She was traveling the road to Heritage Oak for the third time in two days. Each time, it was just a bit more difficult to face the kind of answers she might find there.

Louis would be angry, she had no doubt of it. The man she'd seen yesterday would be furious at being disturbed again—if he spoke to them at all. And Marion... Marion would be hurt, Laurel thought with a flash of guilt. Hurt that she persisted in pursuing something Marion found distasteful and distressing to both herself and her brother.

I won't think about it, Laurel told herself and turned her head to stare, brooding, out the window. What choice do I have? Questions have to be asked, things have to be said. It's gone too far to turn back now. If anything, it should be easier to have the questions come from me. But it wasn't, she thought miserably. Not for any of us.

She knew why Matt was silent. He was giving her time to pull herself together, sort out her emotions for herself before they arrived at Heritage Oak. Considerate. Strange, she thought with a small smile, a week before she'd have sworn Matthew Bates hadn't a considerate bone in his body. She'd learned quite a bit about him in the last few days. Not quite all, Laurel mused, thinking of the paintings in his apartment. But still, a great many important things—the most important of which was that she loved him.

They'd yet to speak seriously about what had happened between them. In an odd way, she felt they'd both been reluctant to probe the other's emotions. Treat it light—don't press. Those were the words that ran around in her head. She wondered if they ran in his as well.

It had all happened so fast. A year? That's fast? she thought with a faint smile. But it had. Whatever had been building between them over the months had been so cleverly ignored that the sudden blaze of passion had been totally unexpected. And that much more exciting. But was that all it was for him? Laurel wished she had the confidence, or the courage, to ask.

Turning back, she studied his profile. Strong, casually handsome with an easygoing smile and amused eyes. Yet he wasn't quite all those things. From his writing she'd already known him to be savvy, ironic, insightful. She'd also discovered that he was only laid-back when he chose to be. That wasn't his true nature. He was an impatient, restless man who simply played the game his own way. Over and above the love that had crept up on her, Laurel had discovered to her own amusement, that quite simply she liked his style.

Partners, she thought as her smile widened. You'd better get used to it, Bates, because we're going to stay that way for a long, long time.

"See something you like?" he asked dryly.

Laurel tilted her head and continued to study him. *Play it light.* The words ran through her mind yet again. "As a matter of fact, I do—and it still surprises me."

He chuckled, and with his eyes on the road reached over and tugged on her hair. "I'm crazy about your compliments, Laurellie. A man never knows if he's been pumped up or slapped down."

"Keeps you on your toes, Bates."

"You did tell me once I had fabulous eyes."

Her brow lifted. "I did?"

"Well, you'd had four martinis at the time."

She laughed as he swung between the pillars of Heritage Oak. "Oh well, who knows what a person might say in that condition? What color are they, anyway?"

He narrowed them as he turned toward her.

"Blue," she said, catching her tongue between her teeth. "Blond hair, blue eyes—rather an ordinary combination, but you do the best you can with it."

"Yeah. And it is a pity about your chin."

Laurel lifted it automatically. "My chin," she said as he stopped the car, "is not pointed."

"I hardly notice it." Matt jingled the keys in his hand as he stepped from the car. He'd lightened her mood, he noticed, but only temporarily. Already, as she glanced up at the house, he could see the struggle between her emotions and her profession. Being Laurel, the profession won, but not without cost.

"Matthew, Marion will see us because her upbringing wouldn't allow her not to, but..." She hesitated as they climbed the porch. "I doubt if Louis will talk to us."

"We'll have to convince him otherwise," he said flatly, and let the knocker fall heavily on the door.

"I don't want to push him too hard right now. If—"

It was the way his head whipped around, the way his eyes flared that stopped her. "When?" he demanded.

She opened her mouth, but the annoyance and impatience on his face had her biting back the first reckless words. "All right," she murmured, turning to face the door again. "All right."

Guilt. He felt the sting and wasn't quite sure what to do about it. "Laurel—"

The door opened, cutting off whatever he might have said. Binney glanced at both of them while a flicker of surprise—and something else—came and went in her eyes. "Miss Laurel, we didn't expect to see you again so soon."

"Hello, Binney. I hope it's not inconvenient, but we'd like to speak to Louis and Marion."

Her eyes darted to Matt, then came back to Laurel. "Mr. Louis has a black mood. It's not a good time."

"Black mood?" Laurel repeated. "Is he ill?"

"No." She shook her head, but hesitated as if the denial had come too quickly. "He is..." Binney stopped as if searching for a phrase. "Not well," she finished, lacing her long bony fingers together.

"I'm sorry." Laurel gave her an easy smile and hated herself. "We won't keep him long. It's important Binney." Without invitation, she stepped into the hall.

"Very well." Laurel caught the quick, accusing glance before the housekeeper shut the door. "Come into the parlor, I'll tell Miss Marion you're here."

"Thank you, Binney." Laurel caught her hand at the entrance to the parlor. "Is Louis often... not well?"

"It comes and goes."

She closed her other hand over the thin hard one as if willing Binney to understand. "Did he have these black moods when Anne was—when he was married to Anne?"

Binney's lips compressed until there was nothing but a tight line. In the way of a woman well used to the house she lived in, and the people she lived with, Binney let her gaze sweep down the hall and up the stairs in a gesture so quick it was hardly noticeable. When she spoke, her words were hurried, low and French.

"You knew him, Miss Laurel, but there have been so many changes, so much pain. Nothing as it was when you came for your tea parties and riding lessons."

"I understand that, Binney. I'd like to help him."

Binney's gaze swept the hall again. "Before," she began, "during the time between when Mr. Charles left and when Mr. Louis brought the girl home, he had many—hard moods. He might roam the house and speak to no one, or lock himself in his study for hours. We worried but..." Her shrug was eloquent. "Later, he began to go away on business and it would be better. The years, they weren't easy, but they were—quiet. Then he brought the girl back, his wife."

"And things changed again?" Laurel prompted.

"Only better." The housekeeper hesitated. Laurel thought she understood perfectly the tug-of-war her loyalties were waging. "We were surprised. She had the look of the first one," Binney said so quietly Laurel strained to hear. "It was strange to see her, even her voice.... But Mr. Louis was happy with her, young again. Sometimes, only sometimes, he would brood and lock himself away."

Ignoring the knot in her stomach, Laurel pressed on. "Binney, was Anne afraid when Louis would—brood?"

Her mouth became prim again. "Perhaps she was puzzled."

"Was she happy here?"

The nut-brown eyes clouded. Her mouth worked before her face became still again. "She said the house was a like a fairy tale."

"And the swamp?"

"She feared it. She should have stayed away. What's there," she said in a low voice, "is best left alone."

"What's there?" Laurel repeated.

"Spirits," Binney said so simply Laurel shivered. There was no arguing with old beliefs, old legends. She let it pass.

"Did Anne see Nathan Brewster often?"

"She was a loyal wife." Her tone changed subtly, but enough that Laurel knew the automatic defense of the estate and all in it had been thrown up. Laurel took what she knew might be the final step.

"Did Louis know that Brewster was in love with Anne?"

"It is not my place to say," Binney replied stiffly and with disapproval. *Or yours to ask.* Laurel heard the unspoken words very clearly. "I'll tell Miss Marion you're here." Coolly, she turned her back on them both and walked away.

"Damn," Laurel breathed. "I've lost her too."

"Sit down," Matt ordered, steering her to a chair. "And tell me what that was all about."

Sitting, Laurel to speak in the flat tone of recital. "She told me that Louis was prone to black moods and brooding after Charles and Elise left. Understandable enough," she added automatically—too automatically for Matt's liking. "The servants worried about him. Then he apparently pulled out of it a bit when he began to travel on business. They weren't expecting him to bring Anne back and obviously her resemblance to Elise caused some talk, but Binney seemed fond of her. She said Louis was happy, less moody, that Anne was happy too."

She sighed, leaning back in the chair, but her fingers drummed on the arms. "She holds to the local feeling about the swamp."

"Ghosts again?"

"Don't be so literal-minded," Laurel snapped. "It's the... essence of the place," she finished lamely.

As Laurel had with the housekeeper, Matt let it pass. "Didn't I hear Brewster's name mentioned?"

"She'd only say that Anne was a loyal wife. I tried to press." She lifted her eyes to his. "That's when I lost her."

"Forget your feelings for a minute and use your head." He spoke sharply because he'd rather face her annoyance than her vulnerability. "If the housekeeper knew about Brewster—and from the way she clammed up she must have—who else knew?"

"You don't hide things from servants, Matthew. They'd all know."

"Yet not one of them mentioned his name when they were questioned by the police."

Laurel linked her hands in her lap to stop her fingers from drumming. "To have mentioned it would've cast a shadow on Anne's reputation and therefore Louis's. Remember too, the investigation led to nothing more than a verdict of accidental death. It would've seemed pointless to stir all that up then."

"And now?"

"The servants are loyal to Louis," she said wearily. "They're not going to gossip to outsiders about something that would bring him more pain."

"I have connections downtown," Matt mused. "I could probably get someone out here to ask a few questions."

"Not yet, Matthew, a few more days." Laurel caught Matt's hand in hers as he stood next to her chair. "I don't want to push the police on Louis until there's no other choice. We don't have enough to justify reopening the investigation in any case. You know it."

"Maybe, maybe not." He frowned down at her and bit back a sigh. "A few days, Laurel. That's all."

"Laurel, Mr. Bates." Marion came in with her hands already extended for Laurel's. "Please, sit down, Mr. Bates. I'm sorry I've kept you waiting, but we weren't expecting you."

Laurel caught the faint disapproval and acknowledged it. "I'm sorry, Marion, I hope we didn't catch you at a bad time."

"Well, I'm a bit pressed, but..." She squeezed Laurel's hands before choosing the brocade love seat across from her. "Would you like some coffee? A cold drink perhaps. It's such a dismal day."

"No, thank you, Marion, and we won't keep you long." Party talk, she thought in disgust. How easy it is to cover ugliness with party talk. "It's important that we speak to you and Louis again."

"Oh." Marion's gaze swept from Laurel to Matt and back again. "Louis is out, I'm afraid."

"Will he be back?" Matt asked her, without accepting her invitation to sit.

"I can't say. That is, I can't say when. I'm sorry." Her expression altered subtly, brow creasing as if she was forced to say something unpleasant. "The truth is, Laurel, I'm not sure he'll agree to talk to you again."

That hurt, but she'd expected it. Laurel kept her eyes level. "Marion, Matthew and I went to see Nathan Brewster yesterday."

They both saw, and registered, each flicker of expression on Marion's face. Distress, agitation, annoyance, doubt; all came quickly and were as quickly gone. "Did you? Why?"

"He was in love with Anne," Laurel returned. "And apparently made little secret of it."

Marion's eyes cooled, the only hint of annoyance now. "Laurel, Anne was a lovely child. Any man might be attracted to her."

"I didn't say he was attracted," Laurel corrected. "I said he was in love with her, in his way. He wanted her to leave Louis."

Laurel saw Marion's throat work before she spoke. The thin gold chain she wore around it glittered with the movement. "What Mr. Brewster may have wanted doesn't mean anything. Anne loved Louis."

"You knew about this." Laurel watched Marion's eyes, pale gray like her brother's.

For a moment Marion said nothing, then the only sound she made was a sigh. "Yes," she said at length. "I knew. It would've been impossible not to see by the way the man looked at her. Anne was confused." Her hands lifted, linked, then fell. "She confided in me because she just didn't know how to deal with it. Anne would never have left Louis," she murmured as her fingers unlinked to knead the material of her skirt. As the nervous gesture continued, her eyes remained level and nearly calm, as if her hands were controlled by something else entirely. "She loved him."

"Did Louis know?"

"There was nothing for him to know," Marion said sharply, then struggled to regain her composure. "Anne only spoke to me because the man upset her. She told her sister that he made her nervous. Anne *loved* Louis," Marion repeated. "What difference does it make now?" She looked at both of them with suddenly tormented eyes, her fingers clutching the filmy material of her skirt. "The poor child's dead and rumors, nasty rumors like this will only make it more difficult on Louis. Laurel, can't you stop this? You must know what this continued pressure does to Louis."

"If things were just that simple," Matt began, breaking in before Laurel could speak. "Why do you suppose someone sent Laurel a warning?"

"Warning." Marion shook her head as her nervous fingers finally stilled. "What warning?"

"Someone left a box on my doorstep," Laurel said with studied, surface calm. "There was a dead copperhead inside."

"Oh my God! Oh, Laurel." She stretched her hands out to grip Laurel's. They trembled ever so slightly. "Why would anyone have done something so nasty? When? When did this happen?"

"Late yesterday afternoon. A few hours after we'd left Heritage Oak."

"Oh, my dear, you must have... Anne was bitten by a copperhead," she murmured as if she'd just remembered. "You think—Laurel, you don't believe that Louis would do such a thing to you. You can't!"

"I can't—I don't want to believe it of Louis," Laurel corrected. "We thought it best if both of you knew about it."

With a steadying breath, Marion released Laurel's hands. "It must have been dreadful for you. My own nerves—Louis's..." She broke off with a shake of her head. "Of course I'll tell him, you know I will, but—"

"Miss Marion?"

Distracted, Marion looked over her shoulder to the doorway. "Yes, Binney."

"Excuse me, but Mrs. Hollister's on the phone, about the hospital charity drive. She's insistent."

"Yes, yes, all right, tell her I'll just be a moment." She turned back, playing with the collar of her dress. "I'm sorry, Laurel, about everything. If you'd like to wait here, I'll take care of this and come back. But I don't know what else I can say."

"It's all right, Marion, go ahead. We'll just let ourselves out."

"Once you put your teeth into it," Matt commented when he was alone with Laurel, "you chomp down nicely."

"Yes, didn't I?" Without looking at him, she picked up her bag and rose. "Professional hazard, I suppose."

"Laurel." Matt took her shoulders until she looked up at him. "Stop doing this to yourself."

"I would if I could," she murmured, then turned away to stare out the window. "I didn't like the way Marion came apart when I mentioned Brewster."

"She knows more than she's saying." He touched her hair, and would have drawn her back against him.

"Louis is outside," Laurel said quietly. "I want to talk to him alone, Matthew."

He took a step back, surprised that such an ordinary request would hurt so much. "All right." When she walked out the French doors, he stuffed his hand in his pockets and moved closer to the window. Without the least compunction, he wished Louis Trulane to hell.

The heat outdoors was only more stifling after the coolness of the parlor. The air tasted of rain, but the rain wouldn't come. What birds that bothered to sing, sang gloomily. She smelled the roses as she passed them and the scent was hot and overripe. As she came closer to him, Laurel could see the damp patches on Louis's shirt.

"Louis."

His head jerked up when she called him and he stopped. There wasn't any welcome in his face or in his stance, nor was there the cool indifference she'd seen the day before. He was furious. "What're you doing here?"

"I have to talk to you."

"There's nothing to say."

"Louis." She took his arm when he started to go on without her. Though he stopped again, he spun back to her with a look that made her drop the hand.

"Leave us both with a few decent memories, Laurel, and stay away from me."

"I still have the memories, Louis, but I have a job to do." She searched his face, wishing there was something she could do, something she could say, to prevent what she knew could be the final breach between them. "I don't believe Anne went into that swamp freely."

"I don't give a damn what you believe. She's dead." He looked over her head, out to the edge of the north lawn where the marsh took over. "Anne's dead," he said again, shutting his eyes. "That's the end of it."

"Is it?" she countered, hardening herself. "If there's the slightest possibility that someone lured or frightened her into that place, don't you want to know?"

He broke off a thin branch of crape myrtle. Laurel was reminded forcibly of Brewster's hands on a pencil. "What you're saying's absurd. No one did—no one would have a reason to."

"No?" She heard the quiet snap of wood between his fingers. "Someone doesn't appreciate our probing into it."

"*I* don't appreciate your probing into it," Louis exploded, tossing down the mangled wood and blossoms. "Does it follow that I murdered my wife!" He spun away from her to stare at the edge of the north lawn. "For God's sake, Laurel. Why do you interfere in this? It's over. Nothing can bring her back."

"Does my interference bother you enough that you'd leave a dead snake on my doorstep?"

"What?" He shook his head as if to clear it. "What did you say?"

"Someone sent me a dead copperhead, all done up nicely in a box."

"A copperhead—the same as . . ." His words trailed off as he slowly turned back to her. "A nasty joke," he said, tossing the hair back from his face in a gesture she remembered. "I'm afraid I haven't been up to jokes of any kind lately, though I hardly see . . ." He broke off again, staring down at her. His expression altered into something she couldn't quite read. "I remember. Poor little Laurel, you were always terrified of them. I nearly strangled that cousin of mine the day he stuck a garter snake under your nose at one of Marion's garden parties. What were you? Nine, ten? Do you remember?"

"I remember."

His face softened, just a little. "Have you outgrown it?"

She swallowed. "No."

"I'm sorry." He touched her face in the first gesture of friendship. She found it hurt more than his angry words. "You never liked the swamp because of them."

"I never liked the swamp, Louis."

"Anne hated it." His eyes drifted back. "I used to try to tease her out of it—just as I used to tease you. Oh God, she was sweet."

"You never let me meet her," Laurel murmured. "Why didn't you let anyone meet her?"

"She looked like Elise." His hand was still on her face, but she knew he'd forgotten it. "It stunned me the first time I saw her. But she wasn't like Elise." His eyes hardened, as slate gray as the sky. "People would've said differently just by looking at her. I wouldn't tolerate it—the comparisons, the whispers."

"Did you marry her because she reminded you of Elise?"

The fury came back at that, so sudden and fierce Laurel would've backed away if his hand hadn't tightened. "I married her because I loved her—needed her. I married her because she was young and malleable and would depend on me. She wasn't a woman who'd look elsewhere. I stayed with her through the year we had so that she wouldn't grow bored and discontent as Elise claimed she had in that damned note."

"Louis, I know how you must feel—"

"Do you?" he interrupted softly, so softly the words hung on the stagnant air. "Do you understand loss, Laurel? Betrayal? No," he said before she could speak. "You have to live it first."

"If there had been someone else." Laurel moistened her lips when she found her mouth was dry. "If there'd been another man, Louis, what would you've done?"

He looked back at her, cool again, icy. "I'd have killed him. One Judas is enough for any man." He turned, walking away from her and the house again. Laurel shivered in the sticky heat.

He'd seen enough. Matt crossed to the French doors and, fighting the urge to go after Louis and vent some of his frustration, went to where Laurel still stood, looking after him.

"Let's go," he said briefly.

She nodded. The mood—hers, Louis's, Matt's—seemed to match the tightness in the air. A storm was brewing in all of them. It wouldn't take much to set it off. In silence, they walked across the neatly trimmed lawn to Matt's car, then drove away from Heritage Oak.

"Well?" Matt touched the car lighter to the tip of a cigarette and waited.

"Binney was right about his mood," Laurel said after a moment. "He's on edge, angry, with nothing to strike out at. He still dismisses Anne's death as an accident. The way he looked out at the swamp..." Laurel glanced up at Matt, seeing the hard, set profile that wasn't so very different from the expression Louis had worn. "Matthew, I'd swear he loved her. He might've gotten involved with her because of her resemblance to Elise, even married her with some sort of idea about having a second chance, but Louis loved Anne."

"Do you think he always kept them separated in his mind?"

"I told you before, I'm not a psychiatrist." Her answer was sharp and she set her teeth. Nothing would be accomplished if she and Matt started sniping at each other again. "I can only give you my own observations," she said more calmly, "and that is that Louis loved Anne, and he's still grieving for her. Part of the grief might be guilt—that he'd teased her about being afraid of the swamp," she told him when he sent her a quick look. "That he didn't take it seriously enough."

"You told him about the box?"

"Yes." Why doesn't it rain? she thought as she pulled her sticky blouse away from her shoulder blades. Maybe the rain would wash everything clean again. "He didn't put it together at first, then when he did, I'd say he was more disgusted than anything else. Then...then he remembered I'd always been terrified of snakes. For a couple of minutes, he was just like he used to be. Kind, warm." Swallowing, Laurel looked out the side window while Matt swore, silently, savagely.

"I asked him why he hadn't let Anne meet anyone. He said he didn't want the comparisons to Elise he knew would crop up. He kept close to her because he didn't want her to grow bored and—"

"Look elsewhere," Matt finished.

"All right, yes." Laurel's head whipped back around. "Aren't you forgetting about those glass houses now, Matthew? Haven't you any compassion at all? Any understanding as to what it's been like for him?"

He met her heated look briefly. "You've got enough for both of us."

"Damn you, Matthew," she whispered. "You're so smug, so quick to judge. Isn't it lucky you never lost anyone you loved."

He hurled his cigarette out the window. "We're talking about Trulane, not me. If you're going to start crusading again, Laurel, do it on your own time. Not when you're my partner. I deal in facts."

She felt the rage bubble up and barely, just barely suppressed it. Her voice was frigid. "All right, then here's another one for you. Louis said he would've killed any man that Anne was involved with. He said it with a cold-bloodedness I'm sure you'd admire. Yet Nathan Brewster still works for him."

"And here's another one." Matt pulled into a parking space at the *Herald* and turned on her. "You're so hung up on Trulane you've made some kind of Brontë hero out of him. You refuse to see him any other way. He's a ruthless, bitter man capable of cold violence. His first wife chose his younger brother. Haven't you ever asked yourself why?"

She jerked her arm out of his hold. "You know nothing about love and loyalty, Matthew."

"And you do?" he tossed back. "If you'd grow up, you'd see that you don't love Trulane, you're obsessed with him."

She paled, and as the blood drained from her face, her eyes grew darker, colder. "I do love him," she said in a low, vibrating voice. "You haven't the capacity to understand that. You want things black and white, Matthew. Fine, you stick with that and leave me the hell alone."

She was out of the car quickly, but he had her by the shoulders before she could dash into the building. "Don't you walk away from me." The anger spilled out, with something very close to panic at the edges. "I've had enough of Louis Trulane. I'll be damned if I'm going to have him breathing down my neck every time I touch you."

Laurel stared up at him, eyes dry. "You're a fool. Maybe you'd better take a good look at the facts again, Matthew. Now leave me alone." When her voice broke, they both swore. "Just stay away from me for a while."

This time when she turned from him, Matt didn't stop her. He waited until she'd disappeared inside the building before he leaned against the hood of his car. With the heat shimmering in waves around him, he drew out a cigarette and tried to pull himself together.

What the hell had gotten into him? He'd attacked her. Matt dragged a hand through his hair. An emotional attack wasn't any prettier than a physical one. The heat? He shifted his shoulders beneath his damp, sticky shirt. That might be part of it, it was enough to set anyone's nerves on edge.

Who was he trying to kid—himself? Matt blew out a long breath and watched the smoke hang in the thick, still air. The crux of it was she'd spent the night with him, giving herself to him, bringing him all the things he'd needed, wanted . . . then he'd seen Louis put a hand to her cheek.

Idiot. Laurel couldn't have cursed him more accurately than he did himself. He'd let jealousy claw at him until he'd clawed at her. He hadn't been able to stop it. No, he corrected, he hadn't tried to stop it. It'd been easier to be angry than to let the fear take over. The fear that he'd had for her since he'd looked in the box on her table—the fear that he had of her since he'd discovered he was hopelessly in love with her. He didn't want to lose her. He wouldn't survive.

Maybe he'd sniped at her hoping she'd back off and let him take over the investigation. If he'd found a way to prevent her going with him into the swamp, she wouldn't have been hurt.

Maybe he'd used Louis as an obstacle because he'd been afraid to risk telling Laurel how he felt about her. He'd planned things so carefully—he always had. Yet things had gotten out of hand from the moment he'd started to work with Laurel on this story. How was he supposed to tell her that he loved her—perhaps on some level had loved her from the moment he'd seen that picture propped against Curt's books? She'd think he was crazy. Matt crushed the cigarette under his heel. Maybe he was.

But he was still a reporter, and reporters knew how to follow through, step by step. The first thing was to give Laurel the space she'd demanded. He owed her that. In giving it to her, he could do a little digging on his own. The next thing was to find a way to apologize without bringing Trulane into the picture again.

The last thing, Matt thought as he crossed the parking lot, the last thing was to get it into her thick head that he loved her. Whether she liked the idea or not.

Chapter Ten

Laurel considered it fortunate that she'd been sent back out on an assignment almost immediately after coming into the city room. She was able to grab a fresh pad, hook up with a photographer and dash out again before Matt was even halfway up on the elevator.

She didn't want to see him, not until the anger and the hurt had faded a bit. The three-car pileup at a main intersection downtown, with all the heat, noise and confusion it would generate, should distract her from her personal problems. Temporarily.

He was being unreasonable, she told herself with gritted teeth while the photographer cruised through a yellow light and joined a stream of traffic. Unreasonable and unyielding. How could anyone be so utterly lacking in compassion or empathy? How could a man who had shown her such unquestioning support and comfort when she'd been frightened feel nothing for someone who'd been through what Louis Trulane had? Didn't he recognize pain? How could she love someone who... That's where she stopped, because no matter how or why, she loved Matt. It was as simple as that.

Because she loved him his lack of feeling and his words had cut that much deeper. To accuse her of being obsessed by Louis. Oh, that grated. Any rational person would understand that Louis Trulane had been her childhood hero. She'd loved him freely, with a child's heart and in a child's way. In the course of time, the love had changed, not because Louis had changed but because she had.

She still loved Louis, perhaps not quite objectively. She loved Louis the way a woman loves the memory of the first boy who kissed her, the first boy who brought her a bouquet. It was soft and safe and passionless, but it was so very sweet. Matt was asking her to turn her back on that memory. Or to dim it, darken it with suspicion.

To a woman like Laurel, the memory of a young man who'd treated a child and her infatuation gently should have no shadows. But Matt was using it to swipe at her for something she couldn't understand. He'd even implied that she might be thinking of Louis when they were together. How could he possibly believe...

Here, her thoughts broke off again as a new idea crept in. A fascinating one. Matt was plain and simply jealous.

"Ha!" Laurel uttered the syllable out loud and flopped back against the car seat. Her photographer sent her a sidelong look and said nothing.

Jealous... well, that was certainly interesting, even if it was still unreasonable and asinine. But if he was jealous, didn't it follow that his feelings for her were more involved than she'd let herself believe? Maybe. Or maybe he was just being typically insufferable—as she'd almost forgotten in the first heady waves of love that he was. Still, it was something to think about.

They had to stop the car in a thick tangle of traffic and bad-tempered blasting of horns. "I'll get out here and go up on foot," Laurel told her photographer absently. "Pull over as soon as you can." Stepping out, Laurel went to work.

Matt was out on the street as well. The noise in the Vieux Carré might have been a great deal more pleasant than what Laurel was dealing with, but the heat was only slightly less intense. He could smell the river and the flowers, a combination that had come to mean New Orleans to him. At the moment, he hardly thought of them. For the past hour, he'd been very busy.

A trip to the police station and a few carefully placed questions had earned him the information that no official search had ever been issued for Elise or Charles Trulane. A missing person's report had never been filed on either of them. The note, the missing clothes and painting gear had been enough to satisfy everyone. Matt wasn't satisfied.

When he'd questioned further, he'd hit a blank wall of indifference. What did it matter how they'd left town or if anyone had seen them? They *had* left, and ten years was a long time. There was plenty of other business in New Orleans to keep the force busy other than an adultery that was a decade old. Sure, the lab boys would play with his little chunk of metal when they had the time, and what was he up to?

Matt had evaded and left with fewer answers than he'd had when he'd gone in. Maybe he'd draw a few out of Curt.

Turning a corner, Matt strolled into a dim little bar where a trio was playing a cool, brassy rendition of "The Entertainer." He spotted Curt immediately, huddled in a corner booth with papers spread all over the table. There was a glass of untouched beer at his elbow. Matt had a quick flashback of seeing Curt exactly the same way during their college days. The smile—the first one in hours—felt good.

"How's it going, Counselor?"

"What?" Distracted, Curt looked up. "Hi." He tipped the papers together in one neat, economical movement and slid them into a folder. "What's up, Matt?"

"The same," he told the waitress, indicating Curt's beer. "A little legal advice," he said when he turned back to Curt.

"Oh-oh." Grinning, Curt stroked his chin, the only resemblance to his sister Matt could see.

"Advice, not representation," Matt countered.

"Oh well." When the waitress put Matt's beer on the table, Curt remembered his own.

"If I decided to add to my portfolio, would you consider Trulane Shipping a wise investment?"

Curt looked up from his drink, his abstracted expression sharpening. "I'd say that was more a question for your broker than your lawyer. In any case, we both know your portfolio's solid. You're the one who gives me tips, remember?"

"A hypothetical question then," Matt said easily. "If I were interested in speculating with a New Orleans-based company, would Trulane be a wise place to sink my money?"

"All right. Then I'd say that Trulane is one of the most solid companies in the country."

"Okay," Matt muttered. He'd figured that one was a blind alley. "Why do you think no one's touched Elise Trulane's inheritance?"

Curt set down his beer and gave Matt a long, level look. "How do you know about that?"

"You know I can't reveal a source, Curt. Fifty thousand," he mused, running a finger down the condensation on his glass. "A hefty principle. Interest over ten years would be a tidy little sum. I'd think even a man like Trulane would find some use for it."

"He doesn't have any claim on the money. It's a straight inheritance in Elise's name." He shrugged at Matt's unspoken question. "The firm handled it."

"And the lady just lets it sit." Matt's brow rose at his own statement. "Strange. Hasn't your firm tried to track her down?"

"You know I can't get into that," Curt countered.

"Okay, let's take it hypothetically again. When someone inherits a large amount of money and makes no claim, what steps're taken by the executors to locate the beneficiary?"

"Basic steps," Curt began, not sure he liked the drift. "Ads in newspapers. In all likelihood an investigator would be hired."

"Say the beneficiary had a husband she wanted to avoid."

"The investigation, any correspondence pertaining to it, would be confidential."

"Mmm-hmm." Matt toyed with his beer as the piano player did a quick, hot rip over the keys. "Did Elise Trulane have a will?"

"Matt—"

"Off the record, Curt. It may be important."

If it had been anyone else, Curt would have brushed it off and found some handy legal jargon to evade the question. He'd known Matt too long and too well. "No," he said simply. "Both she and Louis had wills drawn up, but Elise took off before they were signed."

"I see. And the beneficiaries?"

"Standard wills for husband and wife without issue. Marion and Charles have their own money."

"Substantial?"

"Putting it mildly. Marion's a very wealthy woman." Then, because he anticipated the question before it was spoken, he added, "Charles's investments and his savings sit collecting interest as Elise's do."

"Interesting."

Curt kept his eyes level—not emerald like his sister's but sea green and calm. "Are you going to tell me what all this is about?"

"Just covering all the angles."

"It has something to do with what you and Laurel are working on—for Susan."

"Yeah." Matt swirled his beer as he studied his friend. "You've met Susan?"

"I was out at the house." A faint color rose under Curt's skin, bringing Matt a picture of the time, years before, when Curt had fallen hard for a premed student. "She told me about Anne, and the letters." Curt's gaze came back to Matt's, reminding him that Curt wasn't an impressionable college student any longer, but a man with a sharp legal mind and a quiet strength despite his dreaminess. "Are you going to be able to help her?"

"We're doing what we can on this end. Since you know her, and she's confided in you, maybe you can keep her calm, and out of it, until something breaks."

"I'd already planned on that," Curt said simply. "You taking care of Laurel?"

Matt grimaced, remembering how they'd parted a few hours before. "Nobody takes care of Laurel," he muttered.

"No, I guess not." Distracted again, Curt slipped his folder into his briefcase. "I've got an appointment, but when there's more time, I'd like a few more details on this."

"Okay. And thanks."

Alone, Matt brooded into his beer. Too many loose ends, he mused. Too many pieces that just don't fit. Two people might turn their backs on friends and relatives, especially in the first impetus of love, but not on more money than most people see in a lifetime. Not for ten years.

Either love made them delirious, he concluded, or they're dead. Dead, to him, made a lot more sense.

Leaning back, he lit a cigarette. If they'd had an accident after leaving Heritage Oak, didn't it follow that they'd have been identified? He shook his head as theories formed and unformed in his mind. It all tied together, somehow, with Anne Trulane. And if one of his theories was right, the one he kept coming back to, then someone had killed not once, but three times.

He studied the thin blue wisp of smoke and swore. It was too late in the day to allow a thorough check of Louis's whereabouts on the day of Elise and Charles's disappearance. And tomorrow was Sunday, which meant he probably couldn't get his hands on the information he needed until after the weekend. Monday then, he thought, and crushed out his cigarette. On Monday, no matter how reluctant Laurel was, they would start digging back, and digging thoroughly.

Rising, he tossed bills on the table and strode out. Maybe it was time they had a talk.

Laurel was totally involved with her story when Matt walked into the city room. He started toward her, glanced at the clock, then went to his own desk. Deadline was sacred. When he sat down across from her, he noticed the expression on her face. Unholy glee was the closest he could come.

Laurel nearly chuckled out loud as she dashed off the story. A three-car pileup, a lot of bent metal. Not normally anything she'd have found amusing, but no one had been hurt. And the mayor's wife had been in the second car.

Better than a sideshow, Laurel thought again as she typed swiftly. The mayor's wife had dropped all dignity and decorum and very nearly belted the hapless driver who'd plowed into her from behind, sandwiching her between him and the car stopped at a light in front of her.

The air, already steaming, had been blue before it was over. Maybe it was the heat, or the pressure she'd been under for the last few days, but Laurel found this a much-needed comic relief. It would've taken a stronger person than she not to be amused watching a prim, nattily dressed woman with a wilted corsage grab a man built like a truck driver by his lapels and threaten to break his nose. And that had been before her radiator had blown, spewing water up like a fountain.

Ah well, she thought as she finished up the report, it would do Everyman good to read that people in high places get their fenders dented and their tempers scraped too. Page one, oh yes, indeed.

"Copy," she shouted, glancing at the clock. Just under deadline. Her smile was smug as she turned back and found her gaze linked with Matt's. A dozen conflicting emotions hit her all at once, with one fighting to push aside all the others. She loved him.

"I didn't see you come in," she said carefully and began to tidy the disorder of her desk.

"Just a few minutes ago. You were working." The bedlam of the city room went on around them with shouts of *"Copy!"*, rushing feet and clicking typewriter keys. "Are you finished?"

"Soon as the copy's approved."

"I need to talk to you. Can we have dinner?"

She hadn't expected that cautious, slightly formal tone from him and wasn't sure how to deal with it. "All right. Matthew—" The phone on her desk rang. Still thinking about what she would say to him, Laurel answered, "City room, Laurel Armand."

Matt watched her expression change, the color fluctuate before her gaze jerked back to him. "I'm sorry," she began, indicating the phone on his desk a split second after he'd already started to reach for it. "You'll have to speak up, it's very noisy in here." She heard the faint click as Matt picked up her extension.

"You've been warned twice." It was a whisper of a voice, sexless, but Laurel didn't think it was her imagination that she sensed fear in it. "Stop prying into Anne Trulane's death."

"Did you send me the snake?" Laurel watched Matt punch another extension on the phone and dial rapidly.

"A warning. The next one won't be dead."

She couldn't control the silver shot of panic up her spine, but she could control her voice. "Last night, you were in the swamp."

"You have no business there. If you go in again, you won't come out."

Laurel heard someone across the room yell out a request for coffee, no sugar. She wondered if she were dreaming. "What are you afraid I'll find?"

"Anne should've stayed out of the swamp. Remember that."

There was a click, then the drone of the dial tone. Seconds later, Matt swore and hung up his own phone. "Not enough time for the trace. Any impressions on the voice? Anything you recognized?"

"Nothing."

He picked up her pad, where Laurel had automatically recorded the conversation in shorthand. "To the point," he muttered. "We're making someone very nervous."

Someone, he thought as his own theory played back in his head, who may have killed three times.

"You're thinking about the police again," Laurel decided.

"You're damn right."

Laurel dragged a hand through her hair as she rose. "Listen, Matthew, I'm not saying you're wrong, I just want some time to think it through. Listen," she repeated when he started to speak. "Whoever that was wants us to back off. Well, for all intents and purposes we will be for the weekend. I want some time to go over my notes, to put them together with yours, hash it out. If we do go to the police, on *Monday*," she added with emphasis, "we'd better go with all the guns we have."

She was right, but he didn't like it. Several ideas for nudging her out of the investigation ran through his mind. He'd have the weekend to choose the best of them. "All right, check in with Don. I'll get my notes together."

Instead of the rare steak and candlelight Matt had planned on, they ate take-out burgers and chilling fries at Laurel's drop leaf table. Their notes were spread out— Matt's made up of scribbles Laurel thought resembled hieroglyphics while her own were sketched in precise Gregg shorthand. They hadn't taken the time—and both of them separately agreed it was just as well—to touch on their earlier argument or the reasons for it. For now they were professionals covering every angle of a story.

"I'd say it's safe to assume we have enough circumstantial evidence to conclude that Anne Trulane's death was something more than an unfortunate accident." Laurel wrote in a composition notebook, a valiant attempt to organize their snatches of words and phrases into coherency.

"Very good," Matt murmured. "That sounded like something Curt would say to the jury."

"Don't be a smart aleck, Bates," she said mildly. "Pass me that soda." Taking it, she sipped straight from the bottle and frowned. "We have Susan's claim that Anne was afraid of dark places—the swamp in particular—which has since been corroborated by Louis, Marion and Binney. We have the stolen letters from Susan's hotel room, my nasty little box, a hefty shove in the swamp and an anonymous phone call."

Because she was writing, Laurel didn't notice that Matt snapped the filter clean off his cigarette when he crushed it out. "The first interview with Louis and Marion...nothing much to go on there but emotion, which you don't like to deal with."

"It can be useful enough," Matt said evenly, "when you look at it with some objectivity."

She opened her mouth to hurl something back at him, then stopped. "I'm sorry. I didn't mean to snipe. Brewster," she went on briskly. "We know he thought he was in love with Anne, wanted her to leave Louis. No conjecture there since he said so himself." She underlined Brewster's name heavily and continued. "We also have Marion's corroboration of the first part of that, and Anne's reaction to it. My second interview with Louis leads me to believe that he either didn't know about Brewster's feelings or didn't think they were important enough to worry about, as Brewster's still employed by his company."

Laurel rubbed a hand over the back of her neck, the first and only outward sign that she was tired. "The gist of it is that we agree it seems unlikely Anne would've gone into the swamp without some kind of outside pressure—and that it's less likely she would have continued to head deeper unless she had no choice. In my opinion, Brewster's still the obvious candidate."

Matt flipped over his pad to a new set of notes. "I spoke with Curt today."

"Huh?" Laurel looked up at him, trying to tie his statement with hers.

"I wanted some corroboration on a theory I had."

"What does Curt have to do with this?"

"He's a lawyer." With a shrug, Matt lit a cigarette. "As it turns out, I was luckier than I expected as he works for the firm that handles Elise Trulane's inheritance."

Laurel put down the bottle she'd lifted. "What does that have to do with any of this?"

"I'm beginning to think quite a lot. Listen." He skimmed through his notes. "Fifty thousand dollars, plus ten years interest, has never been touched. Charles Trulane's money sits moldering. Untouched. There would've been a very discreet, and I'm sure very thorough investigation on behalf of the bank to locate them." He flipped back a few pages, then lifted his eyes to Laurel's. "No missing person's report was ever filed on either Elise or Charles Trulane."

"What're you getting at?"

Very carefully, he set down his pad. "You know what I'm getting at, Laurel."

Needing to move, she rose from the table. "You think they're dead," she said flatly. "Maybe they are. They could've had an accident, and—" She broke off, and he knew her thoughts had followed the same train his had. Laurel turned back to him, her eyes very steady. "You think they were dead before they left Heritage Oak."

"It's more than a possibility, isn't it?"

"I don't know." Pressing her fingers to her temples, she tried to think logically. "They could've taken off, changed their names, gone to Europe or the Orient or God knows where.''

"Could've," he agreed. "But there's enough room to doubt that, isn't there?"

"All right, yes." She took a deep breath. "And if we go that route, figuring they were tied with Anne's death somehow, it'd put Brewster in the clear. But why?" Laurel demanded. "Who'd have had a motive but Louis, and he was out of town."

"Was he?" Matt rose, knowing they had to read carefully around Louis Trulane. "He has his own plane, doesn't he? Flies himself—or did. You know what the possibilities are there, Laurel."

She did. An unexpected arrival, the lovers caught, unaware. A moment's madness. In a small private plane the bodies could've been taken anywhere. Pale, she turned back to face Matt. He was expecting her to argue, or to back out. Of course, she could do neither one now.

"It won't be easy—maybe impossible," she added in a calm, professional voice, "to check the incoming and outgoing flights on a night ten years ago."

"I'll get started on it Monday."

She nodded. "I'll work on Curt. We might be able to get the name of the firm that looked for Elise and Charles."

"No."

"No?" she repeated blankly. "But it makes sense to try that angle if we're going at it this way."

"I want you to back off." He spaced his words very evenly as he rose. "I don't want you asking any more questions."

"What the hell are you talking about? You don't get a story without asking questions."

"Whatever we get out of this, whatever the outcome as far as the paper is concerned, we'll split down the middle. But from now on I take over."

Laurel tilted her head. "You're out of your mind."

Maybe it was the very calm, very mild way she said it that tripped the last button. Every reasonable argument, every carefully thought-out method of persuasion deserted him. "I'm out of *my* mind!" he threw back. "That's rich." He paced, deliberately walking away from her so that he wouldn't just grab her by the collar and shake. "It's not a game, damn it. We're not playing who can hit page one."

"I've never considered my profession a game."

"I don't want you in my way."

Her eyes narrowed. "Then I'll stay out of it. You stay out of mine."

"It's dangerous!" he shouted. "Use your head. You're the one who's been hit on, not once, but three times. Whoever's behind Anne's death isn't going to hesitate to kill again."

Her brow lifted—that damned, beautiful, haughty black brow. "Then I'll have to watch my step, won't I?"

"You idiot, no one called me and told me to back off. No one threatened me." There was panic in his voice now, raw panic, but she was too busy fuming to notice.

"You want to know why, Bates?" she hurled out at him. "Because I'm a woman and obviously would buckle under. The same way you figure if you shout enough and throw your weight around I'll do the same thing."

"Don't be any more stupid than you have to."

"But the one thing they forgot," she continued furiously, "the one thing *you* forgot, is that I'm a reporter. And to get a story, to get the truth, a reporter does what's necessary. Most of us deal with being in jeopardy in one form or another. That's the business."

"I'm not in love with most reporters," Matt tossed back. "I'm in love with you!" He stormed right past her as he said it, not stopping until he'd reached the table and his cigarettes.

Laurel stared at him while he pushed aside papers in search of a match. She was winded, as though she'd raced up flight after flight of stairs two at a time. Now that she'd reached the top, she simply forgot why she was in such a hurry in the first place. It wasn't until he'd stopped swearing and muttering to turn to her that she felt the glow, the warmth, the pleasure.

Matt set down the unlit cigarette and stared at her. What the hell had he said? Oh God, had he just blown everything by laying his cards on the table before he'd covered his bet? And just how was he going to handle this one? He decided to give her a way out if she wanted one.

"Did I—just say what I think I said?"

Laurel didn't smile, but folded her hands neatly in front of her. "Yes, I have a witness."

His brow lifted. "There's no one here."

"I'll bribe someone."

He hooked his hands in his pockets because he wanted so badly to touch her. "Is it what you want?"

She gave him an odd look, then took a step closer. "I wonder why I thought you were insightful and observant. It's a general sort of rule, Matthew, that when a woman's in love with a man she likes it better if he's in love with her too."

His heartbeat was very light and fast. He couldn't remember ever feeling like that before. "Tell me," he murmured. "Don't make me beg you."

"Matthew..." A little dazed that he couldn't see what must have been glowing on her face, she reached for him. "You're the only man I've made love to because you're the only man I've been in love with. Neither of those things is ever going to change."

"Laurel." But he couldn't say more because her mouth was on his, giving, just giving. His arms came around her to draw her closer as thoughts spun in his head. So long— it's been so long. He could hardly remember a time when he hadn't wanted it to be like this. A time when he hadn't wanted to have those words still lingering on the air. "Again," he demanded. "Tell me again."

"I love you. Only you." Her arms curved up his back until she could grip his shoulders. "I thought if I told you before, even an hour ago, you'd think I was crazy. When?" Giddy, she clung to him. "When did it start?"

"You wouldn't believe me." Before she could disagree, his lips were on hers again.

He took her deep, and still deeper, quickly. If he'd thought he'd loved her to the point of madness before, it was nothing compared to what stormed through him now. His love was met, and matched. Everything was washed from his mind but Laurel.

She could lose herself in a kiss from him, lose herself in that soft, velvet-edged darkness he'd first taken her to. To know that he wanted her was exciting. To know that he loved her was glory. Words, there were so many words she wanted to say. But they would wait until this first overriding need was satisfied. As she felt her bones melting, she drew him with her to the floor.

Quickly, quickly. Neither spoke but both knew the other's mind. Hurry. Just to feel one another's flesh. Clothes tangled, untangled, then were discarded. Oh the sweetness of it, the sweetness that came from only a touch. She could smell the hot muskiness of the day on him with the lingering scent of soap. She wallowed in it with her lips pressed against his throat. His pulse beat there, fast and light.

He murmured against her ear, only her name, but the sound of it drifted through her softly. The slow, liquefying pleasure made everything she'd ever felt before seem hollow. Then his tongue dipped inside to follow her name.

A long lingering stroke, a whispering caress. There was no need to hurry now. Passion was filled with wonder. I'm loved, I'm wanted. Spirits are fed on this alone. She could feel it pouring from him—contentment—even as his heartbeat hammered against hers. Desire, when mixed with such emotions, has more power. And at times, more patience. They'd woo each other.

His lips moved over her shoulder, down, lazily down to linger on the pulse point at the inside of her elbow. She felt the answering beat from a hundred others. Her hand ran through his hair, the curling thickness of it, before she let her fingers stroke beneath to his neck. He lifted his head to look at her and the look held—long, silent—until, smiling, their lips joined again.

The change happened so slowly perhaps neither of them noticed. Not yet urgent, not yet desperate, but desire grew sharper. Gradually, quiet sighs became quiet moans. With his mouth at her breast he heard her breathing quicken. His senses were clouded—her scent, her taste, the satin that was her skin. Hunger seeped into them, and the excitement that came from knowing the hunger would be satisfied. His hands journeyed down.

The inside of her thighs was as warm and alluring as velvet. He let his fingers linger there, then his mouth. Though she shuddered, the first crest came easily, a gentle lifting up and up, a quiet settling. Her body throbbed with anticipation of the next while her mind was filled with him. Head whirling, she shifted to lie over him, to give to him all the pleasures he'd given to her.

How warm his flesh was, how firm his body. Her hands wandered down to his hips, skimmed over his thighs. She felt the quiver of muscle beneath her.

She was floating, but the air was thick and syrupy. Her limbs were weighted, but her head was light and spinning. She felt him grasp her, heard him hoarsely mutter her name. Then he was inside her and the explosion went on and on and on. She had only enough sanity left to pray it would never stop.

He watched her. He struggled to hold back that seductive darkness so that he would always have this image of her. The light fell over her brilliantly. With her head thrown back, her hair streamed down her back. She knew only pleasure now—his pleasure. He held her there for an instant with perfect clarity. Then the darkness, and all its savage delights, overcame him.

Chapter Eleven

It was dark. Matt had no idea of the time, and cared less. They were snuggled close in Laurel's bed, naked and warm. Like careless children, they'd left their clothes in heaps in the living room. It was pleasant to imagine they could stay just as they were for the whole weekend—dozing, making love, saturating themselves with each other.

He knew all there was to know about her, what pleased her, what annoyed, what made her laugh. He knew where she'd come from, how she'd grown up, snatches of her childhood that he'd drawn out of Olivia or her father and Curt. She'd broken her ankle when she'd been nine and had worked on her high school paper. She'd slept with a one-eared stuffed dog until she was seven.

It made him smile to think of it, though he wasn't certain she'd be pleased to learn he knew.

There was so much he hadn't told her. Matt could remember the hurt on her face when he'd pushed her questions away. There was so much he hadn't told her—but she loved him anyway.

Laurel shifted against him, her eyes open and adjusted to the dark, her body quietly content. "What're you thinking?"

He was silent for a moment, then lifted a hand to touch her hair. "I grew up in that painting." Laurel put her hand in his and said nothing. "Old people stayed off the street at night and anyone else traveled in groups. Too many alleys and broken streetlights. Cops patrolled in pairs, in cars. I can't remember a night when I didn't hear the sirens.''

She was so warm and soft beside him. The room was so quiet. Why was he bringing it all back? Because it never really goes away, he answered himself. And I need to tell her.

"I worked for a guy who ran a newsstand. One summer we were robbed six times. The last time he was fed up enough to put up a fight. I was out of the hospital in two days, but it took him two weeks. He was sixty-four."

"Oh, Matthew." Laurel pressed her face into his shoulder. "You don't have to talk about it."

"I want you to know where I came from." But he fell silent again as two long minutes passed. "In the apartment where I lived, the halls smelled of old cooking and sweat. It never went away. In the winter it was cold, drafts through the windows, icy floors. In the summer it was a furnace. You could smell the garbage from the alley three floors down. At night you could hear the street—dealers, prostitutes, the kids who looked for both. I stayed away from the dealers because I wanted to stay healthy and used the prostitutes when I could scrape up the extra money."

He waited, wondering if he'd sense her withdrawal. Her hand stayed in his. Laurel was remembering her impression of his apartment. He'd made an art out of comfort. How much he must have hated growing up without the basic rights of warmth and security. And yet... he'd brought the painting with him. He hadn't forgotten his roots, nor was he ignoring that part they'd had in forming him. Neither would she ignore them.

"I lived with my aunt. She took me in when my mother died and my father took off. She didn't have to." He linked his fingers with Laurel's. "She was the most unselfish person I've ever known."

"She loved you," Laurel murmured, grateful.

"Yes. There was never enough money, even though she worked too hard and when I was old enough I brought in more. The rent would go up in that filthy place or..." He broke off and shrugged. "Life," he said simply. "I swore I was going to get us out of there. One way or the other I was going to get us the hell out. I knew what I wanted to do, but it was like pie in the sky. A reporter, a job on one of the big New York papers and a salary that would move her out to some nice little place in Brooklyn Heights or New Rochelle.

"So I ran copy and studied until my eyes hurt. There were other ways," he murmured, "quicker ways to get the kind of money I wanted, but that would've destroyed her. So when the scholarship came I took it, and I got out. When I'd come back during the summer, it was so hot I'd forget what it was like to live in that place in January. By the middle of my senior year I had nearly enough saved to move her out—not to a house in Brooklyn Heights, but to a decent apartment. By that summer I'd have gotten her out. She died in March."

Laurel turned her head so that her lips could brush over his skin, lightly, easily. "She would've been proud of you."

"If I'd have taken another way, she might still be alive."

"If you'd have taken another way," Laurel said slowly, rising on her elbows to look at him, "you'd have killed her yourself."

His eyes glinted in the filtered light of the moon. "I've told myself that, but other times I think I might've given her even six months of comfort." He caught Laurel's hair in his hand, feeling the fine silk of it. "She used to laugh.

Somehow, she'd always find a way to laugh. I owe her just for that."

"Then so do I." Lowering her head, she kissed him. "I love you, Matthew."

"When I've thought of you, and me, I've wondered how the hell I was going to work it." He cupped the back of her neck. "We couldn't have had more different beginnings. There were times I thought I wanted you just because of that."

When she lifted her head, he was surprised to see her smiling. "You ass," she said lovingly.

"So beautiful," Matt murmured. "I'll never forget that picture Curt had of you, the one he kept on his desk in our room."

Surprised, Laurel started to speak, then stopped. He'd said she wouldn't believe it; now, with emotions swamping her, she didn't want to tell him he'd been wrong. She wanted to show him.

"I could see you at one of those long, lazy garden parties in a silk dress and picture hat," Matt said softly. "It made my mouth water. And I could see you with someone bred for the same things."

"I hate to repeat myself," she began, but he didn't smile. "You're thinking of Louis," Laurel said flatly.

"No." He started to draw her back to him. "Not tonight."

"You listen to me." The humor and the softness had fled from her eyes as she pulled away. "The way I feel about you has nothing, *nothing* to do with the way I feel about Louis. I've loved him since I was a child and in almost exactly the same way. Both he and Marion were an intricate, vital part of my childhood. The fairy-tale part, every girl's entitled to one."

He remembered her grandmother saying essentially the same thing. The muscles in his shoulders began to relax. "I think I understand that, Laurel. It's today that concerns me."

"Today my heart aches for him, for both of them. Today I wish I could help, knowing, at the same time, that what I have to do might hurt them beyond repair. If my feelings had been different, don't you think that sometime over the last ten years, I'd have gone to him? I wonder why," she said heatedly before he could answer, "when I waited all these years to fall in love, I had to fall in love with an idiot."

"The luck of the draw, I guess."

"Well, I'll tell you one thing, Bates, I'm not going to explain myself to you on this again. Take it or leave it."

He let out a deep breath and paused as if weighing the pros and cons of the ultimatum. In the dim light he could see the angry glare in her eyes, the agitated rise and fall of her shoulders. She might've been molded in a softer manner than he, but no one matched wits or wills so well.

"Will you marry me, Laurel?" he asked simply.

He heard the quick hitch of her breath, saw the surprise rush into her eyes. For a moment, there was quiet. "It took you long enough," she said just as simply, then dived onto him.

Laurel awoke with the sun streaming over her face and Matt nibbling on her ear. She didn't have to open her eyes to know it was a beautiful day. Sometime during the night the rain had come to wash the heaviness from the air. Without opening her eyes, she stretched and sighed. Matt's lips moved to her jawline.

"I love the way you wake up," he murmured. He slid a hand down to cradle her hip.

"Mmmm—what time is it?"

"Morning." His lips finally found hers.

With another lazy stretch she linked her arms around his neck. "Have I ever told you how much I like you to kiss me just like that?"

"No." Lowering his head, he did so again while she lay boneless beneath him. "Why don't you?"

"If I tell you—mmmm—you'll know how to win every argument."

Laughing, he pressed his lips to the curve of her shoulder. "I'm crazy about you, Laurellie. When're we getting married?"

"Soon," she said definitely. "Although the minute we tell Grandma she'll—" Laurel broke off, eyes flying open. "Oh God, *brunch!*"

"I wasn't thinking of food just yet," Matt murmured, going back to nibble on her ear.

"Oh no, no, you don't understand. What time is it?" Shoving him aside, Laurel grabbed the bedside clock. "Oh boy, we'd better get moving or we'll be in serious trouble."

Matt grabbed her around the waist as she started to hop out of bed. "If we stay right here," he began, pinning her beneath him again, "we can get into serious trouble by ourselves."

"Matthew." Laurel avoided the kiss, but it landed on the vulnerable hollow of her throat. "Sunday brunch at Promesse d'Amour is sacred," she said unsteadily.

"Can you cook?"

"What? Oh, well yes, that is, if your stomach's very broad-minded you could almost call it that. Matthew, don't." Breathless, she caught his wandering hand in hers.

"Why don't we have a private brunch here, somewhere around dinner time?"

"Matthew"—she shook her head to clear it, then put both hands firmly on his shoulders. "Since you're going to join the family, you might as well get used to certain ironclad rules and traditions. Sunday brunch," she continued when he grinned, "is nothing to play around with."

"I'm an iconoclast."

"Bite your tongue," she told him and struggled with a grin of her own. "Grandma would forgive me if I took up exotic dancing. She'll even overlook the fact that I'm marrying a Yankee, but she'd never, never let me get away with missing Sunday brunch. Even being late clouds the reputation and we're pushing that."

Matt gave a long, exaggerated sigh. "For Miss Olivia then," he agreed and let Laurel wiggle out from under him.

"I'm going to get a shower," she said, dashing toward the bathroom. "If we move fast, we'll make it before deadline."

"Two can shower as quick as one," he commented as he stepped in with her.

"Matthew!" Laughing, Laurel lifted a hand to his chest. "If we're in here together we're definitely going to be late for brunch."

He drew her against him. "I'll risk it."

"Matthew—"

"You forget." He lowered his mouth to nibble on hers. "I know how to win arguments."

"Oh damn," she sighed and melted against him.

They were late.

"We're really in for it," Laurel muttered as Matt turned the car under the arched cedars.

Matt sent her a quick wolfish grin. "It was worth it."

"Just get that cat-ate-the-canary look off your face, Matthew," Laurel warned. "Try to look suitably humble."

"We could use the one about the flat tire," he suggested.

"No less than a five-car pileup equals pardon," she said grimly. "And you don't have a dent in this car." She shot him a look.

"No," he said positively, "not even for you."

"It's that practical Yankee streak," she said under her breath as the house came into view. "Okay, it probably won't work, but we'll go for it. Turn your watch back."

"Do what?"

"Turn your watch back, fifteen minutes." She fussed rapidly with her own. "Go on!"

"What's she going to do?" he demanded as he parked his car beside Curt's. "Take you to the woodshed?"

"You'd be surprised," Laurel muttered. "Oh-oh, here she comes. Listen, I know this might be almost impossible for you, Matthew, but look innocent."

"Maybe I'll just drop you off here and see you back in town."

"You do and I'll break your arm," she promised as she stepped from the car. "Grandma!" Laurel went forward with smiles and open arms. She kissed both lined cheeks and pretended she didn't notice the coolness in the sharp emerald eyes. "You look wonderful."

"You're late," Olivia said flatly.

"Oh no, minutes to spare. I've brought Matthew with me," she added quickly. With luck, a lot of it, it would be enough to distract Olivia.

"Miss Olivia." He took the haughtily offered hand and lifted it to his lips. "I hope I'm not intruding."

"You're late," she repeated while her gaze raked over both of them.

"Why, how could we be?" Laurel countered, glancing down at her watch. "It's only just eleven now."

"That trick's older than I am." Olivia lifted her chin in the manner her granddaughter had inherited. "*Why* are you late?" she demanded, daring either of them to make an excuse.

Laurel moistened her lips. If she had a few more minutes she could probably come up with a great lie. "Well, you see, Grandma—"

"It's my fault, Miss Olivia," Matt put in, earning a grateful glance from Laurel.

"What," Olivia began regally, "does my granddaughter being late have to do with you?"

"I distracted her in the shower," he said easily.

"Matthew!" Laurel cast him a horrified look that altered into one that promised swift and lethal revenge. His name echoed off into silence.

"I see." Olivia nodded. "That's a reasonable excuse," she decreed as Laurel's mouth dropped open. "Close your mouth, girl," she said absently as she continued to study Matt. "Took your own sweet time about it, but that's worked out for the best. You'll be marrying her soon."

It wasn't a question. Matt could only grin as Laurel began to sputter. "Very soon," he told Olivia.

"Welcome to the family"—she grinned and offered her cheek—"Yankee." With a wink for her granddaughter, she held out a hand for Matt to formally escort her around the house to the terrace.

No one's like her, Laurel thought with a fierce flurry of love and pride. Absolutely no one.

With her usual panache, Olivia dominated the table, with her son at the opposite end and the younger generation between them. As always, she'd made the most out of the Sunday tradition. White linen, gleaming silver and crystal, fresh flowers in bowls that had been treasured before the war.

The talk was quiet, general, easy. Laurel could see that Susan was a much different woman from the one who had fallen apart outside the city room. No more trembling fingers. If there was a sadness in her eyes, it was fading. She cast Laurel one look that spoke of complete trust. With it, Laurel felt the burden grow.

Not now, she told herself as she sipped at cool, dry champagne. Tomorrow was soon enough to bring all that back. For today, she needed to absorb the magic and the timelessness. Where else, she wondered, could six people be sitting with the sun gleaming on silver that was more than a century old? There was birdsong and a precious breeze that might only last a moment. It was too rare to crowd with sorrows and suspicions. And she was in love.

She glanced over at Matt, and her eyes told him everything.

"This will be your job one day, Laurellie," Olivia stated, cutting delicately into the crêpe on her plate. "Traditions like this are important—more for the children than their parents. You and Matthew are welcome to the west wing when you're married. Permanently or whenever you feel the need to come. The house is big enough so that we won't bump into each other."

"Have some more coffee, mother," William interrupted, sending her a telling look on his feelings about matchmaking. "I want to talk to both of you." He nodded to his daughter and to Matt. His glance barely skimmed over Susan, but it was enough to tell Laurel he was referring to Anne Trulane. "Monday morning, my office."

"Business is for Monday." Olivia sent her son back a look every bit as stubborn. "I want to talk about the wedding. The garden couldn't be better suited to a summer wedding. You're welcome to have it here on the terrace."

"How about next weekend?" Matt put in, reaching for his coffee.

"Matt, don't encourage her," William advised. "She'll have Curt suing you for breach of promise."

"Damn right!" The thought made Olivia give a hoot of laughter as her hand came down on Laurel's. "We've got him now, Laurellie. William!" She caught him in the act of smothering a laugh with a cough. "Aren't you going to ask this boy all the rude questions a father's supposed to ask? A father can't be too careful when a man wants his daughter—especially a Yankee."

"The truth is," Laurel began before her father could speak. "Matthew's marrying me for the house, and as a cover so he can dangle after Grandma."

Her father's grin altered into blank astonishment. "Are you joking?"

"No," Laurel said lightly as she dipped a strawberry into cream. "Matthew's crazy about Grandma."

"Laurel—" William began with a half laugh, only to break off without any idea what to say.

"She's not joking," Curt murmured, studying his sister. He glanced over at Matt as he remembered his roommate's fascination with a photograph, the questions. "All this time?" he said softly.

"Yes." Matt looked over at Laurel and smiled. "All this time."

"Well, it's been a cleverly kept secret," her father stated. "And from a veteran bloodhound like me."

Smiling, Laurel reached out a hand to him. "Do you mind?"

He gripped her hand. "Nothing could please me more." His gaze shifted to Matt. "Nothing. The point is"—his fingers relaxed with his smile—"I didn't think the two of you even liked each other. You had one particular adjective for Matt, as I recall."

"Insufferable," Laurel supplied. "It still holds."

"That's what adds spice to a relationship," Olivia declared as she pushed back from the table, a signal that meant the formality of the brunch was over. "Susan, be a sweet child and run up to my room. There's a small locket in my jewelry case, gold, encrusted with pearls."

The moment she'd gone, Olivia turned to Curt. "Going to let this Yankee show you up, Curtis?"

Rising, Curt made a great to-do over removing a piece of lint from his jacket. "Ma'am?"

"*He* lollygagged around for a year. I expect you should be able to snatch that girl up in half the time."

"Mother." William strolled over to place a hand on her shoulder. "Be satisfied with one victory."

"After I'm through with Curtis," she continued irrepressibly, "I'm getting started on you."

He acknowledged this with a nod before he turned to his son. "Every man for himself. Ah, Matt, there's something I've been meaning to talk to you about."

"Coward," Olivia murmured as her son drew Matt away.

"Is this it, Miss Olivia?"

"Yes, thank you." She smiled as Susan handed her the locket. "Curtis, why don't you take Susan through the garden. You like the garden, don't you, Susan?"

"Yes." Susan looked down at her hands, then lifted her eyes to Curt's. "Yes, I do."

"There, you see, she likes the garden. Run along. Now then." Without pausing for breath, she turned to Laurel.

"Grandma." Laurel gave her a long, hard hug. "I adore you."

Olivia let herself enjoy the warmth and scent of youth before she drew Laurel away. In her own masterly way she studied her granddaughter. "You're happy."

"Yes." With a laugh, Laurel tossed back her hair. "If you'd have asked me a month ago—good God, a week ago—how I'd feel about marrying Matthew Bates on the terrace, I'd've said..." She broke off, laughing again. "I'd better not repeat what I'd've said."

"You pretended you weren't attracted to him right from the beginning."

"I did a good job of it."

Olivia gave a hoot. "Ah, but you're like me, child!"

"The highest of compliments."

Olivia dropped the locket into her lap and took Laurel's hands. "When we love, really love, it's with everything we have, so we don't give it easily. Your grandfather..." She looked misty for a moment, young. "God, but I loved that man. Fifteen years with him wasn't enough. When he died, I grieved and grieved hard, but then life—you have to live it as it comes. The others, after him, they were..." She shook her head and smiled again. "They were for fun. I cared about every man I've been with, but only one had all of me. You'd understand that," she murmured. "So would your Yankee."

"Yes." Laurel felt the tears swim into her eyes and blinked them back. "I love you, Grandma."

"You'll lead each other a dance," Olivia said after giving Laurel's hands a quick squeeze. "There's nothing better I could wish for you. This is for you now." Olivia lifted the locket from her lap, cupping it in her hand a moment as if warming it. "Your grandfather gave it to me when we were engaged. I wore it when I married him. It would mean a great deal to me if you wore it when you marry Matthew."

"Oh Grandma, it's lovely." Laurel took the gold, gleaming dully and still warm from her grandmother's hands. It was studded with tiny pearls that carried just a hint of blue under the white. "I've never seen you wear it."

"I haven't since he died. It's time it was worn again and worn by a bride."

"Thank you." Leaning over, Laurel kissed Olivia's cheek, then with a smile turned the locket over in her palm. So lovely, she thought, and it would look so perfect against a floaty, romantic white dress. Maybe something with lace and...

As memory jarred, she pressed a hand to her temple.

"Laurellie?"

"No." Absently she patted her grandmother's hand. "I'm all right, I've just remembered something. Or think I have. I have to use the phone."

Jumping up, she dashed into the house with the locket clutched in her hand. From memory, she dialed Heritage Oak. With her eyes on the locket in her hand and her mind on another, she barely heard the answering voice.

"Oh Binney," she said quickly. "It's Laurel Armand." When there was silence, she leaped into it. "Please, Binney, I know you're angry with me for questioning you, I understand. I'm sorry, truly sorry if I pressed too hard."

"It isn't my place to be angry with you, Miss Laurel," she said quietly. "It isn't my place to answer questions."

"Please, there's something I have to know. It could be very important. A locket." She plowed on into the unreceptive silence. "The locket Louis gave Elise before they were married. She wore it on her wedding day, and I think, always after that. I can remember that I never saw her when she wasn't wearing it. The gold locket with the etch-

ing on the front. Do you remember it, Binney? You must,"
she went on before there could be an answer. "She kept
Louis's picture in it."

"I remember the locket."

Something—not excitement, not fear—began to pound
in her chest. Laurel recognized it as disillusionment. "She
always wore it, didn't she? It was very small and elegant,
something she could wear every day and still wear with
evening clothes."

"It was her habit to wear it."

Laurel swallowed and fought to keep her voice steady.
"Binney, was Elise afraid of the swamp?" She knew the
answer herself, but wouldn't go with childhood memories
now. It was time for facts no matter how they hurt.

"It was a long time ago."

"Please, Binney. You knew her, you were there."

"She did not like it," Binney said flatly. "She knew the
legend."

"But sometimes—sometimes—she went in there,"
Laurel whispered.

"Yes, sometimes she went in, but only with Mr. Louis."

"Yes, yes, I know." Laurel let out a long breath. "Only
with Louis. Thank you, Binney."

Hanging up, Laurel stared down at the locket in her
hand. She slipped it gently in her pocket and went to find
Matt.

He saw her, crossing the lawn. With a brief word to her
father, Matt went to meet her. Even from the distance,
he'd recognized the look in her eyes. "What is it, Laurel?"

Her arms went around him, her cheek to his chest. For
a moment, she just needed that—the strength, the promise. The tug-of-war inside her was almost over. It didn't
surprise her that she still loved Louis, or the Louis she'd

known. "Matthew, where's the piece of locket you found in the swamp?"

"I took it to the police lab. They're going to run some tests." He drew her away far enough so that he could see her face. "Why?"

Quietly, she drew a breath. Then she straightened and stood on her own. "They're going to find that it was out in the weather, perhaps covered and uncovered by rain and dirt over and over—for ten years."

"Ten—" He broke off as understanding came. "It was Elise's."

"I remembered where I'd seen it. I just called Heritage Oak and spoke to Binney to be sure. Elise wore that locket every day."

Because she was pale, because he loved her, Matt chose to play devil's advocate. "All right, but it's still not proof. She could've lost it in there any time."

"No, it's not proof," Laurel agreed. "But I don't think there's a chance that Elise simply lost it there. First, it was too important to her. And second, she didn't go in there often. She wasn't afraid the same way Anne was, but she had a healthy respect for the legend. The only times she went in, she went in with Louis. Binney just corroborated."

He could see the struggle, the emotion, in her eyes. This time he felt none of the frustration, the jealousy that had plagued him. Gently, he cupped her face in his hands. "I'm sorry, Laurel."

She caught his wrists in her hands and held tight. "Oh God, Matthew, so am I."

"I think we should fill in your father before we leave," he said carefully. "But we might want to keep it away from Susan for a while. We still don't have anything solid for the police."

"No." Laurel glanced over as she heard Susan's laugh drift from the garden. "Let's leave her out of it for now. My father can probably put on enough pressure to reopen the investigation on Anne, and stir one up on Elise and Charles."

"We've got enough," Matt agreed, watching the struggle on her face, "to start putting pressure in the right places."

"Oh God, Matthew, do you realize, if what we're thinking is fact . . . Louis must be terribly ill. With Charles and Elise it might have been a moment of blind fury, but all these years it would've eaten at him. And then to meet Anne." She pressed her fingers to her eyes. Would she ever be able to separate the emotion from the necessity? "He needs help, Matthew. Can you imagine what a dark place he's been living in all this time?"

"He'll get help. But, Laurel." He took her shoulders until she dropped her hands and looked at him. "First we have to prove it. I think if we concentrate on the first—on Charles and Elise," he said carefully, "it'll lead to Anne. It's not going to be easy for you."

"No," she agreed, "not easy, but necessary." Watching his eyes, she thought she could almost see the idea forming. "What're you thinking, Matthew?"

"Pressure," he murmured. "The right pressure in the right place." He brought his attention back to her. "Louis must already be on the edge, Laurel, ready to go over. He's warned you off three times. Just what do you think his reaction would be if he saw that piece of locket?"

"I think—" Laurel's hand reached automatically for the one in her pocket—"it would break him."

"So do I." He slipped an arm around her shoulders. "We'll have to make another trip to Heritage Oak tomorrow."

Chapter Twelve

The clutter of notes was still spread over Laurel's drop leaf table with the wrappers and cardboard of their take-out meal. Clothes—hers and some of his—were scattered over the floor. Laurel closed the door behind them and jiggled her keys in her palm.

"You're a slob, Matthew."

"Me? It's your place. Besides"—he nudged his shirt out of his way with his foot and sat down—"you were the one who dragged me to the floor, crazy for my body. And," he continued when she snorted, "you were the one who pulled me out of here this morning like the building was on fire."

He was distracting her—she was distracting him—from what hovered around the verges of both their thoughts: Louis Trulane and what to do about him.

"Well, since I've already had your body, and brunch," she added sweetly, "you can help me clean up this mess."

"Better idea." Rising, he yanked her into his arms. "Let's add to it."

"Matthew!" But his mouth crushed down on hers. His fingers were making quick work of the zipper at the back of her dress. "Stop it!" Half-laughing, half in earnest, she struggled against him. "You're crazy. Don't you ever think about anything else?"

"Sometimes I think about eating," he confessed, then nipped, none too gently, at her collarbone.

"Matthew, this is ridiculous." But the quick heating of her blood told her otherwise. "It was only a few hours ago that—oh."

"I'm hungry again," he murmured, then devoured her mouth.

God, he was making her head spin. With her dress already down to her waist, Laurel tried to pull away. "Stop. There's things we have to talk about, and—"

"Mmm, a reluctant woman." He dragged her against him again. "That gets my lust cells moving."

"Your what?" she demanded, choking on a laugh.

"Just watch." Before she realized what he was up to, she was slung over his shoulder.

"Bates! Have you lost your mind?"

"Yeah." He pulled the dress the rest of the way off as he headed for the bedroom. Carelessly, he dropped it at the doorway, sending her shoes to follow. "Blame it on the lust cells."

"I'll tell you what I think about your lust cells," she began, but the wind rushed out of her as she landed on the bed beneath him.

Then he was taking her back to places she'd been, but so swiftly, so immediately, she couldn't keep up. Relentless, he wouldn't allow her to fall behind. Bright streams of color seemed to burst inside her head while her body was consumed with pleasure, such hot, liquid, throbbing pleasure.

No thought. No words. She could only feel and feel and feel. The rest of her clothes were gone. Had she heard something rip? Did it matter? Her body was wild to be touched, tasted, to experience all the mad things he seemed determined to do.

Emotions exploded in her, poured out of her. Oh God, she was so free, so wonderfully free. Pleasure was an absence of pain and she felt only pleasure in his hands, his lips, the taste of his tongue inside her mouth, the feel of his flesh beneath her fingers.

Excitement, heady, steamy excitement. Liberation. Soaring, half-crazy with delight. The knowledge that her life would be splashed with moments like this made her laugh aloud. The next moment he had her gasping. She locked her arms around him as her world rocked and spun.

He took her on a roller coaster of sensations, plummeting down, climbing, climbing, only to whip blindly around a turn to fall again. Weightless, helpless, with the air rushing in her lungs and her heart thundering in her ears.

Then he plunged into her, driving her over that last, giddy hill.

When she could breathe again without gasping, when she could think without pooling all her concentration onto one word, Laurel slid a hand across his chest. He was lying on his back, possibly, she thought, just possibly as enervated as she.

Laurel turned her face into his shoulder. "You did that more for me than yourself."

Matt gave a weak laugh. "I'm a real samaritan. No lengths I won't go to to serve my fellow man."

"Matthew." Laurel shifted, so that she lay over him, her head supported just under his by her folded arms. "You knew I was tense, trying not to be. You knew I didn't want to think about what's going to happen, even though I have to. I was being a coward."

"No." He brushed the hair back from her face. "You were being human. You needed to wipe it away for a little while, blank it out. I did too." He smiled, with the touch of irony in the lifted brow. "This was better than an aspirin."

She managed to match the smile. "You'll have to keep yourself available every time I have a headache." She

lowered her face to kiss his chest, then lifted it again.
"Matthew, I can handle this. I can."

Maybe, he thought. Maybe not. But he'd give her the
first test. "Okay. I want to run over to the lab and get the
locket back whether it's been tested yet or not. I'd feel
better if I had it."

Laurel nodded, accepting. "And in the morning, we
take it out to see Louis."

I take it out, he corrected silently, but merely nodded.
That was something he'd deal with when the time came.
"If he doesn't just fall apart at that, we'll have a lot of
legwork to do, but we bring the uniforms in."

"Agreed," she said simply. Her heart was already numb.

He sat up, wondering just where he'd tossed his clothes.
"Do you want to come with me now?"

"No." She let out a deep breath. What had her grandmother said? Life—you have to live it. "I'll tell you what
I'm going to do for you, Bates, and believe me, you're the
first man I've offered this to."

He was standing, pulling on his slacks. The grin tilted.
"Fascinating."

"I'm going to cook you dinner."

"Laurel, I'm—overwhelmed."

"You might be a great deal more than that after you eat
it," she murmured.

"We could always eat out."

"Don't be a coward," she said absently, wondering just
what she had in the freezer that could be used. "Better pick
up some wine." Kneeling, she buttoned up the rest of his
shirt for him herself. "And some bicarbonate," she added,
laughing up at him.

"Bicarbonate," he murmured. "That doesn't inspire
confidence."

"No, but it'd be a smart move."

"I shouldn't be long."

"Take my door key in case I'm involved in the kitchen. And, Matthew," she murmured, sliding her arms around his neck. "Make sure you control those lust cells until you get back."

He kissed her, then gave her a friendly pat on the bottom. "An hour," he promised before he strolled out.

An hour, Laurel mused, and stretched her arms to the ceiling as she heard the front door close. That should give her time enough to try her hand at being domestic.

It didn't take her long to deal with the disorder of the apartment, or to realize just how smoothly Matt had eased out of helping. She decided that having to eat her cooking would be punishment enough for him. Going to the kitchen, she poked in the refrigerator.

A little juice, less milk, two pounds of butter. *Two* pounds, Laurel mused. How had that happened? Still, there was the makings for a salad in the vegetable bin. A start. Maybe a casserole, she decided. She was almost sure she had a cookbook around somewhere.

Fifteen minutes later, she was elbows deep in the beginnings of a tuna-and-macaroni dish that the cookbook promised was foolproof. With a glance around the now cluttered and disarranged kitchen, she smirked. Whoever wrote the book didn't know Laurel. She was going over the next step when the phone rang.

Matt, she thought, dusting off her hands as she went to answer. He probably wants to know if I'd like him to pick up some take-out Chinese. You're not getting off that easy, Bates. Grinning, she answered.

"Hello."

"Oh, Laurel, thank God you're home."

Tension banded the back of her neck immediately. "Marion? What is it?"

"Laurel, I didn't know what to do. Who else to call. It's Louis."

"Is he hurt?" Laurel asked quickly. "Has he been hurt?"

"No—I don't know. Laurel…" Her voice broke and she began to weep.

"Marion, calm down and tell me what's happened."

Her breathing rasped into the phone. "I've never seen him this bad before. All day, he wouldn't speak to anyone, but that happens sometimes. Oh God, Laurel," she said on a sudden burst of emotion, "it's been such a strain, worse since Anne…Laurel," she began again, nerves quivering in her voice. "I need help."

"I'm going to help," Laurel said as calmly as she could. "What's happened?"

"Just now, a few minutes ago." Laurel heard her take a steadying breath. "He flew into a rage. He wasn't—wasn't making any sense. He was saying things about Elise, and about Anne. I don't know—it was as though he'd gotten them mixed up in his mind."

Laurel pressed her lips together. She had to be calm, had to think straight. "Where is he now?"

"He's locked himself in his room. He's raging up there, I can hear the furniture…Laurel, he won't let me in."

"Marion, call a doctor."

"Oh God, Laurel, don't you think I've tried that before? He won't see one, and he's never been as—as out of control as this. Please, come. You were always our friend. Louis was so close to you before—before all of this. You might be able to calm him down, and then if I could just figure out what to do so that he'd—he'd get help," she finished in a whisper. "Laurel, please, I just can't expose him to strangers the way he is now. I don't know who else to trust."

"All right, Marion." She pictured Louis locked in his room, on the edge of madness. "I'll be there as quickly as I can."

"Laurel . . . as a friend, not as a reporter, please."

"As a friend, Marion." After hanging up the receiver, Laurel pressed the heels of her hands to her eyes.

Matt shifted the bag he carried and slipped Laurel's key into the lock. "I got red and white," he called out. "You didn't say what we were having." A glance at the living room showed him that Laurel had already tidied up. He was going to hear about that, Matt mused, grinning. "I don't smell anything burning."

He swung into the kitchen and lifted a brow. Whatever she as making, it apparently required every inch of counter space. Matt set the wine in the sink—the only place left for it—and shook his head. This was the woman whose notes were always in perfect order? Whose desk was clear and ordered at the end of each day? Dipping his hand into a bowl he drew out a cold, spongy elbow of macaroni.

"Ah, Laurel," he began, dropping it again. "There's this little place on Canal Street, great seafood. Why don't we..." He paused at the entrance to the bedroom. Empty. He felt the first prickles of unease. "Laurel?" Matt repeated, pushing open the bathroom door. Empty. Fear washed over him; he pushed it back. She'd just gone out for something she was missing for the recipe. She probably left a note.

When he hurried back into the living room, he found it by the phone. But even before he read it, he didn't feel relief, only more fear.

Matthew—Marion phoned, very upset. Louis is losing control, talking about Elise and Anne. He's locked himself in the bedroom. She needs help. I couldn't say no. Laurel.

"Damn it!" Matt tossed down the note and raced for the door. The fear was still with him.

Shadows were lengthening as Laurel turned down the drive toward Heritage Oak. The air was still again in the late afternoon hush. A bird called out, as if testing the silence, then was quiet again. Even as she stopped the car at the end of the drive, Marion was running down the front steps toward her.

Her hair was loose, her face pale and tear-stained. It ran through Laurel's mind quickly that she'd never seen Marion so totally lacking in composure.

"Oh God, Laurel." Marion grabbed her as if she were a lifeline. "I couldn't stop him. I couldn't stop him!"

Laurel's head whipped up, her eyes fixing on the window of Louis's room. She had a sickening picture of him lying dead by his own hand. "From what? Marion, what has he done?"

"The swamp. He's gone in the swamp." She covered her face with her hands and sobbed. "I think he's lost his mind. The things he was saying—he pushed me."

Not dead, Laurel told herself. Not dead. You have to be calm. "What did he say?"

Marion lowered her hands. Her eyes were wide, stricken. "He said," she began in a whisper, "he said he was going to find Elise."

"Elise," Laurel repeated, forcing herself not to give in to the horror of it.

"We have to do something!" Marion grabbed her again. "Laurel, we have to do something, go after him—*find* him. He's having a breakdown or—"

"Marion, how can we find him in there? We should call the police."

"*No!* Not the police. It's Louis." She seemed to come to grips with herself as she released Laurel. "I can find him. I know the swamp as well as he does. You don't have to come with me—I asked too much."

Laurel dragged both hands through her hair as Marion started across the lawn. He'd put her up on her first pony, she remembered. Played patient games of chess, listened to her rambling stories. Whatever he'd done, how could she walk away without trying to help?

"Marion, wait. I'm coming with you."

Marion stopped and held out a hand.

They moved quickly toward the swamp. The instant revulsion came as she stood at the edge of it, but she forced it back. It was just a place, she told herself. And Louis was in it.

The shadows were long on the ground now. Daylight was thinning. They'd have an hour, maybe a bit longer, Laurel reassured herself, before it was too dark to see. By then, they'd have found him. She moved into the swamp without hesitation.

"I think he might have gone to the river—to where Anne was found." How much did Marion know or suspect, Laurel wondered. At the moment, she didn't think Marion was in any shape for questions or theories. "Are you going to be all right?" she asked, looking at Marion's flowing pastel skirts and elegant pumps. "It's hard going through here."

"It doesn't matter," Marion said impatiently. "Louis is my brother."

"It's going to work out for the best," Laurel told her, almost believing it herself.

"I know." Marion managed a smile.

They moved slowly, side by side, and then with Laurel just ahead as the path narrowed. The place was alive with noise—birds, insects. Once she saw a blue heron rise up gracefully and glide. They were coming to the river.

"Maybe we should call to him, let him know we're here," Laurel suggested. "It might frighten him if we're too quiet."

"He won't hear you."

"Not if he's gone the other way, but if he's anywhere near the river, then—" Laurel broke off as she turned around.

Marion held a gleaming old gun in her hand. A sliver of sunlight dashed against the chrome. For a moment, as her gaze rested on it, Laurel's mind went blank. Then slowly, she looked up into Marion's face. Despite the red-rimmed eyes, the tracks of tears and disordered hair, her expression was calm and composed. There was something buzzing in her ears that Laurel didn't yet recognize as terror. She kept her eyes on Marion's face.

"Marion." The name came out calmly enough. Calmly and very soft. "What are you doing?"

"What I have to do," she said mildly.

Was the gun for Louis? Laurel thought frantically. If it was for Louis, then why was it pointed at her? She wouldn't look at it—not yet—she'd look only into Marion's clear gray eyes. "Where's Louis, Marion? Do you know?"

"Of course, he's working in his study. He's been working all afternoon."

"All afternoon," Laurel repeated, trying to hold back the trickle of fear that was eating at her wall of control. "Why did you call me?"

"I had to." Marion smiled, a gentle one. "After I spoke to you this morning about Elise's locket, I knew it had gone too far. You'd gone too far."

"Spoke to me? But I talked to Binney…" She trailed off. "It was you?"

"I'm surprised you didn't remember that Binney spends her Sundays with her sister. You made it terribly simple, Laurel. You expected Binney, so I was Binney." The smile faded. Marion's brows drew together, delicately, as they did when she was annoyed. "I'm very disappointed in you,

Laurel. I warned you to stay out of this. Can you imagine the trouble you'd have caused if it had been Binney? Questioning a servant about family matters." She shook her head as a flicker of irritation darkened her eyes. "You've been raised better than that."

Raised better? Laurel thought giddily. Was she mad? Oh God, she thought as fear washed over her. Of course she was mad. "Marion, what are you going to do?"

"You'll have to be punished," Marion told her calmly. "Just like the others."

Matt's car skidded to a halt next to Laurel's. He hadn't stopped cursing since he'd tossed her note aside. Cursing helped hold off the fear. If he's hurt her, Matt thought as he sprinted up the steps. By God, if he's touched her... Lifting a fist, he pounded on the door.

"Trulane!" He pounded again, sick with fear. When the door opened he was through it in seconds with his hands gripping hard on Louis's shirt. "Where's Laurel?"

"What the hell do you think you're doing?" Louis stood rigid, his eyes burning with fury.

"What have you done with Laurel?" Matt demanded.

"I've done nothing with Laurel. I haven't seen her." He looked down at the hands gripping his shirt. "Get your hands off me, Bates" He'd like a fight, Matt realized. He'd like the simple release of a purely physical explosion—fist against flesh. Matt saw it in his eyes.

"We'll go a few rounds, Trulane," Matt promised grimly. "There's nothing I'd like better—after you tell me what you've done with Laurel."

Louis felt something bubbling inside of him. The emotion, for the first time in weeks, had nothing to do with grief. It was pure fury. Somehow it was cleansing. "I told you I haven't seen her. She isn't here."

"You can do better." Matt flung a hand toward the open door. "Her car's out front."

Louis followed the gesture and frowned. Some of the pent-up anger gave way to puzzlement. "She must've come to see Marion."

"Marion called her." Matt shoved him back against the wall, catching him off-balance. "She told her to come because you were out of control, locked in your room."

"Are you crazy?" Louis pushed him away and they stood eyeing each other, both tall men, both ready, anxious, for blood. "Marion would hardly call Laurel if I were locked in my room. As it happens, I've been working all afternoon."

Matt stood, breathing fast, trying to hold on. If he hit Trulane, just once, he might never stop. He could feel the violence bubbling up inside him. Not until he saw Laurel, he promised himself. And after that . . .

"Laurel left me a note that she was coming here after a phone call from Marion concerning your unstable condition."

"I don't know what the hell you're talking about."

"Laurel's car's out front," Matt said between his teeth. "And you're here."

Louis gave him a cold stare. "Perhaps you'd care to search the house."

"I'll do just that," Matt tossed back. "While I'm at it," he continued as he reached in his pocket, "why don't you take a look at this and see what explanation you can come up with.

Opening his palm, he held out the piece of locket. Louis gripped his wrist, fingers biting into flesh. "Elise—where did you get that?" His eyes whipped up to Matt's, dark, tormented. "Where in hell did you get that?"

"In the swamp." Matt closed his hand over it. "Laurel recognized it too, then confirmed it with your housekeeper on the phone this morning."

"Binney?" Louis stared down at Matt's closed hand. "No, Binney isn't here. The swamp? In the swamp?" Again Louis lifted his head. His face was white. "Elise never went in there without me. She always wore that, always. She had it on the day I left for New York, before she—" He shook his head, color rushing back to his face. "What the hell are you trying to do?"

Matt tried to take it step by step. A new fear was crawling in. "Laurel told me she called here—around noon—and spoke with your housekeeper."

"I tell you Binney isn't here, hasn't been here all day! She goes to her sister's. All the servants are free on Sundays. There's only Marion and I."

"Only Marion?" Matt murmured. Marion who had called—Marion who had, by her nervous distress, sent them after Brewster. And Marion, Matt remembered all at once, who had said Anne told Susan that Brewster made her nervous. How would she have known that unless— unless she'd seen the letters. "Where is she?" Matt demanded, already halfway down the hall. "Where's your sister?"

"You just wait a damned minute." Louis grabbed Matt by the arm. "What are you getting at? Where did you get that locket?"

"In the swamp!" Matt exploded. "Damn you, don't you understand Marion's got her!" His face became very still and very pale. "In the swamp," he repeated. "She has her in the swamp, just like the others."

"What others?" Louis was on him before Matt could move. *"What others?"*

"Your sister's a murderer," Matt flung back at him. "She's killed three times, and now she has Laurel."

"You're crazy!"

"I'm not crazy." He opened his fist again so that the locket sat dully in the center of his palm. "We were in the swamp the other night—someone attacked her. The same person who sent her the dead snake, and the one who threatened over the phone yesterday. The same person," he said evenly, "who called her here now. Laurel came here for you," Matt told Louis, watching his eyes. "Are you going to help me?"

Louis stared down at the locket, his breath unsteady. "We'll go in. Wait here."

Turning, he walked into a room across from the parlor. Seconds later, he came back with a small pistol. The color had drained from his face again. In silence, he handed it to Matt. "She's taken the gun." His eyes met Matt's. "The antique we've kept under glass."

Don't panic, don't try to run. Laurel ran the words over and over in her mind as she watched Marion. *She looks so calm now, as if any minute she'd smile and offer me tea and cakes. How long has she been mad?* Laurel swallowed slowly, careful to make no movement at all. *Talk— she wants to talk about it.*

"Punish," Laurel repeated. "You punished the others, Marion?"

"I had to."

"Why?"

"You were always a clever child, Laurel, but not clever enough." She smiled again, old friend to old friend. "After all, look how easily I threw your attention onto Brewster just by telling the truth. Anne would never have left Louis. She adored him."

"Then why did you punish her, Marion?"

"She shouldn't have come back." Marion let out a little, shuddering sigh. "She should never have come back."

"Come back?" Laurel repeated, allowing herself a quick glimpse over Marion's head. If she could distract her, get just a few seconds' head start, could she lose herself in the brush?

"She didn't fool me," Marion said, smiling again. "Oh, she fooled the rest of them—especially Louis—but I knew. Of course, I pretended I didn't. I'm very good at pretending. She was afraid of the swamp," Marion said absently. "I knew why, of course I knew why. She died here before, she had to die here again."

Laurel stared as the horror of what was in Marion's mind washed over her. Keep talking, keep talking, keep talking, she told herself as a thrush began to sing in the cypress behind her. "Why did you kill Elise the first time?"

"She had no right!" Marion exploded so that Laurel gave a quick, involuntary jerk back. "She had no right to the house. It was mine, always it's been mine. Louis was going to will it to her. To *her!* She didn't have Trulane blood, wasn't one of us. *I'm* the oldest," she raged. "By rights, the house was mine. Father was wrong to leave it to Louis."

Her chest began to shudder, but when Laurel looked down, she saw the gun was still steady. "It's always been mine. I love it. All of this." Her eyes skimmed the swamp and softened. "It's the only thing I've ever loved."

"But why Elise?" Laurel interrupted. A house, she thought frantically. Did someone kill for a house, a plot of grass and dirt? It had been done before, she reminded herself. Over and over again, since the caves. "Why didn't you kill Louis, Marion? Then you'd have inherited."

"Laurel." Her voice was soft. "Louis is my brother."

"But—but Charles," she began.

"I never wanted to hurt Charles." Tears sprang and swam in her eyes. "I loved him. But he saw us, he interfered." A single tear drifted down her cheek. "I didn't have a choice. Elise and I went for a walk—she was lonely without Louis. When we were far enough away from the house I took out the gun. This gun," she said, lifting it higher. "Do you recognize it, Laurel?"

She did. She'd seen it under glass in the library. The same gun another Trulane had used to kill—to punish. "Yes."

"I knew I had to use this." She ran a fingertip down the barrel. "It was as if it was waiting for me, as if someone was telling me that it was right that I punish Elise with this. Do you understand?"

"I'm trying to."

"Poor Laurel," Marion murmured. "Always so understanding, so caring. That's how I knew you'd come today when I called."

Laurel felt her knees start to shake. "You were telling me about Charles."

"Yes, yes. He saw us, you see. Saw me leading Elise into the swamp at gunpoint. At least, he must have—I didn't have time to ask, everything happened so quickly. We were here when he found us. Just here."

She glanced around as if they might not be alone after all. Laurel took a very slow, very small step to the right. "Don't, Laurel," Marion murmured, lifting the gun a fraction higher. Laurel stood still. "Elise went wild—that must be when her locket was broken. I should've been more careful. I had to shoot her. Then Charles was pushing me down. My own brother—shouting at me. The gun seemed to go off again, all by itself. Then he was dead."

Her tears were dry now, her eyes clear. "I didn't now what to do at first, and then, it just came. They'd been lovers, like the other two who'd died here. I'd have to forge another note. This time Elise would tell Louis she'd left him for Charles. It was better," she muttered. "Really, it was better that way. I had to drag them to the quick-sand.''

"Oh God." Laurel closed her eyes, but Marion didn't notice.

"I packed some of their clothes. All the servants were gone because it was Sunday. Charles's paints too—I nearly forgot them. Of course, he'd never have left without his paints. They went in the quicksand too. Then it was done. It was simple. Of course, Louis was hurt. He suffered." Her eyes clouded for a moment. "I know he blamed himself, but I could hardly tell him it was all for the best. The house was mine again, he was busy with his work. But sometimes," she whispered. "Sometimes I'd hear them in here. At night."

Laurel swallowed the metallic taste of horror. "Charles and Elise?"

"I'd hear them—it would wake me up and I'd have to come out, come look. I never saw them—" Again, she looked around as if expecting someone. "But I heard."

It's driven her mad, Laurel thought. How is it no one saw, no one suspected? She remembered Marion at a charity function only months before—delicate, elegant with a spray of violets pinned to her lapel. She looked down at the gun again.

"Then she came back," Marion said flatly. "She said her name was Anne and Louis believed her. I knew. She'd look at me with those soft, shy eyes, and she was laughing! I let her think she'd fooled me."

"And you brought her in here again."

"I had to be more careful this time. Louis hardly let her out of his sight and she'd never, never go near the swamp. That night, he was working late. I heard her in the study with him. He told her he'd probably be a couple hours more, to go up to bed without him. I knew it was time. I went into her room, put a pillow over her face. Oh, I had to be careful, I couldn't kill her then. It had to look like an accident this time. She was very small, and not strong. It only took a minute until she was unconscious. Then I carried her out here."

Marion smiled, remembering. "I had the gun, but she didn't know I couldn't afford to use it. When she came to, she was terrified. Elise knew she was going to die again. She begged me to let her go, but I made her get up. I thought it best if she drowned in the river. When she started to run, I let her. It would be simpler if she exhausted herself first and I kept close. Then I heard her scream. The snake, a young one, Elise had walked right over the nest. You see, it was meant," Marion told her. "It was right. All I needed then was enough time for the poison to work—and a night, a whole night out in that damp air. I waited until she stopped running, until she was unconscious, here, right here where she'd died before. Then I went home." Marion smiled, but now her eyes were blank. "She won't come back this time."

"No," Laurel said quietly. "She won't come back."

"I've always been fond of you, Laurel. If you'd only listened, this wouldn't have happened."

Laurel moistened her lips and prayed her voice would be steady. "If you shoot me, Marion, they'll take you away from Heritage Oak."

"No!" Her hand tightened on the gun, then relaxed. "No, I'm not going to shoot you, unless I have to. If I do, I'll have to place the blame on Louis. I'll have to, you'll be responsible for that."

It was so hard to breathe, Laurel discovered. So hard to make the air come in and go out. If she concentrated on it, she'd keep herself from screaming until Marion made her stop. "I won't walk into the river, or the quicksand for you."

"No," Marion agreed. "You're not like the others, not so easily frightened. But there's one thing..." Holding the gun level, she sidestepped toward the wild cane. "You came in here to snoop around, you couldn't leave it alone. And you met with a tragic accident. Just like Elise—Anne." She drew a wicker hamper out of the bush. "This one," she said quietly, "isn't dead."

She knew, and the fear wrapped around her. Tight. With a long, smooth stick, Marion pushed the hamper closer, then flicked off the lid. Laurel froze, feeling the weightlessness in her head, the ice in her stomach as the snake slithered out. Then another one.

"I didn't want to take any chances," Marion murmured. Setting down the gun, she held the stick with both hands. She looked up at Laurel and smiled. "You've always been terrified of them, haven't you? How well I remember you fainting dead away over a little garter snake. Harmless creatures." She poked her stick at the copperheads until they coiled and hissed. "These aren't."

She wanted to run, to scream. The gun would've been better. But her voice was trapped by the fear, her legs imprisoned by it. As if her consciousness had floated off, she felt her skin spring damp and clammy.

"It won't matter if you don't move," Marion told her easily. "They're angry. I can make them angrier." She prodded them again, nudging them closer to Laurel. One lashed out at the stick and Marion laughed.

It was the laugh Matt heard. It chilled him to the bone. When he saw them, the snakes were less than a foot away from Laurel, hissing, coiling, enraged, as Marion continued to prod at them. Matt gripped the gun in both hands, prayed, and fired.

"*No!*" Marion's scream was long and wild as the body of one snake jerked, then lay still. She spun around, stumbling, not even feeling the fangs that sank into her ankle before Matt pulled the trigger again. And she ran, bursting through the wild cane like an animal, hunted.

"Laurel!" Matt had his arms around her, dragging her against him. "You're all right." Desperate, he closed his mouth over hers. "It's over. I'm getting you out."

"Matthew." The sobs were heaving in her chest and she fought against them. "She's mad. She killed them all—all of them. My God, Matthew. The snakes—"

"Gone," he said quickly, pulling her closer. "They're gone. You're all right."

"For the house," Laurel said into his chest. "Dear God, she killed them for the house. Louis—"

Matt turned his head. Only a few yards away, Louis stood staring at them. There was no color in his face. Only his eyes seemed alive. "She's been bitten," Louis said so quietly Matt barely heard. "I'll go after her."

"Louis—" Matt looked back at him, finding there was nothing, absolutely nothing that could be said. "I'm sorry," he murmured.

Nodding, Louis walked into the cane. "Just get Laurel out of here."

"Come on." Matt pressed his lips to her temple. "Can you walk?"

"Yes." The tears were streaming down her face, but she found them a relief. "Yes, I'm all right."

"When I'm sure of that," he said as he held her close by his side, "I'm going to strangle you."

He waited until they were in the clear, then drew Laurel down on the grass. Her head sank to her knees. "I'll be all right in a minute, really. We'll have to call the police."

"Louis took care of it before he left the house. They'll be here any minute. Can you tell me now?"

At first, she kept her head on her knees as she spoke. Gradually, as the horror and the dizziness faded, she lifted it. When she heard the sirens, her hand slipped into Matt's and held tight.

So much confusion—with the police in the swamp, all the questions. A hell of a story, Laurel thought on a bright bubble of hysteria. Though she swallowed it, she gave into the need to press her face into Matt's shoulder. Just a few more minutes, she told herself. I'll be all right in just a few more minutes. She let Matt lead her back to the house, then drank the brandy he urged on her.

"I'm better," she told him. "Please, stop looking at me as though I were going to dissolve."

He stared at her a minute, then, pulling her into his arms, buried his face in her hair. "Damn you, Laurel." And his voice trembled. "Don't ever do that to me again. I thought I was too late. Another five minutes—"

"No more," she murmured, soothing him. "No more, Matthew. Oh, I love you." She drew his face back. "I love you so much."

She met the aggressive kiss, feeling all the fears drain. He was here, holding her. Nothing else mattered. She lifted a hand to his face as the front door closed. "It's Louis," she said quietly.

He came in slowly. His hair and clothes were streaked and disheveled. His eyes, Laurel saw, weren't cold, weren't remote, but weary and vulnerable. Without hesitation, she rose and went to him. "Oh, Louis."

He slipped his arms around her, holding on. His face dropped to the top of her head. "We found her. She's— they're taking her to the hospital, but I don't know if... She's delirious," he managed and drew away. "Did she hurt you, Laurel?"

"No, no, I'm fine."

His gaze shifted to Matt. "I owe you much more than an apology."

"No, you don't."

Louis accepted this with a nod and walked to the brandy. "Are you up to telling me the whole story now?"

He kept his back to them as Laurel related everything Marion had said. Once, when she saw his shoulders shudder, she faltered. He shook his head and gestured for her to finish.

"I need to talk to Susan," he said when Laurel fell silent.

"She's with my grandmother."

Pouring another brandy, Louis nodded. "If she'll see me, I'll go out tomorrow."

"She'll see you Louis," Laurel murmured. "Please, please don't take the blame for this."

He turned around slowly. "Do something for me?"

"Of course, you know I will."

"Yes," he said with a faint laugh. "Yes, I know you will. Write your story," he said in a stronger voice. "And make it good. Everything, I want everything out. Maybe then I can live with it."

"Matthew and I'll write it," Laurel told him and rose to take his hand. "And you'll live with it, Louis. I'm coming back and see that you do." She touched his cheek. "I love you."

With a ghost of a smile, he kissed her. "You're well matched with him, Laurel," he murmured, looking over at Matt. "You're as stubborn as he is. Come back," he agreed, squeezing her hands. "I'm going to need you."

When they walked from the house a few minutes later, Laurel breathed deep. Just the scent of night. The scent of life. "It's beautiful, isn't it?" She threw her face up to the stars. "We'd better call my father, let him know we have one hell of an exclusive on the way."

"Next time you decide to go for one," he said dryly, "remember we're partners. No more solo meets."

"You got it," she agreed. "Let's take your car," she decided, too keyed up to drive. "I can get mine tomorrow. Oh God, Matthew!" Dropping down inside, she leaned back against the seat. "I never want to go through another night like this, even for a Pulitzer."

"That's what you get for taking off before you fixed dinner." His hands were finally steady, he noted as he turned the key. "Makes a man wonder what kind of wife he's getting."

"A gem," she assured him. "You're getting a gem, Bates." Leaning over, she kissed him. "I haven't thanked you for saving my life."

"No." He smiled, cupping the back of her neck so he could linger over the kiss. "What'd you have in mind?"

"Doing the same for you." She grinned at him. "We're eating out."

* * * * *

COMING NEXT MONTH FROM

NORA ROBERTS

#23 SUMMER DESSERTS

When hotel owner Blake Cocharan hired dessert chef Summer Lyndon, he didn't expect more than his taste buds to be stimulated. But Summer had all the ingredients he'd been looking for—and a few that he didn't expect!

#24 THIS MAGIC MOMENT

Mysterious magician Pierce Atkins tried to get the skeptical and lovely Ryan Swan to believe in the power of the unknown. He knew he had to convince Ryan that his love was no illusion—but could he compel her to trust him long enough to create that magic moment?

AVAILABLE NOW:
#21 PARTNERS
#22 SULLIVAN'S WOMAN